Kristy and the Haunted Mansion

**Other books by
Ann M. Martin**

Rachel Parker, Kindergarten Show-off
Eleven Kids, One Summer
Ma and Pa Dracula
Yours Turly, Shirley
Ten Kids, No Pets
Slam Book
Just a Summer Romance
Missing Since Monday
With You and Without You
Me and Katie (the Pest)
Stage Fright
Inside Out
Bummer Summer

BABY-SITTERS LITTLE SISTER series
THE BABY-SITTERS CLUB Mysteries
THE BABY-SITTERS CLUB series
(see back of the book for a more complete listing)

Kristy and the Haunted Mansion
Ann M. Martin

AN
APPLE
PAPERBACK

SCHOLASTIC INC.
New York Toronto London Auckland Sydney

Cover art by Hodges Soileau

ISBN 0-590-44958-3

12 11 10 9 8 7 6 5 4 3 2 1   3 4 5 6 7 8/9

Printed in the U.S.A.   28

First Scholastic printing, June 1993

The author gratefully acknowledges
Ellen Miles
for her help in
preparing this manuscript.

Kristy and the Haunted Mansion

CHAPTER 1

"Merrily we roll along, roll along, roll along — "

"Row, row, row your boat — "

"Jingle bells, Santa smells, a million miles away — "

My head was pounding. I felt as if I were trapped in a hot, tiny room with nine munchkins who were all singing different songs. And in a way, I was. The tiny room was a van, which my big brother Charlie was driving along the highway. It was hot because — well, because it was a hot, muggy day. The munchkins were nine little kids who make up a softball team that I co-coach. And those kids were singing nine different songs, all at the same time.

"Comet, it makes your mouth turn green — "

"Doe, a deer, a female deer — "

"Boys are made of greasy, grimy gopher guts — "

I looked over at Bart Taylor, the other coach. He had pressed his hands over his ears. He grinned at me and shrugged.

"A hundred bottles of pop on the wall — "

"The wheels on the bus go round and round — "

"The itsy-bitsy spider climbed up the waterspout — "

I couldn't take it anymore. But what could I do? The kids were just bursting with energy. They were probably also a little nervous about the game they were going to be playing that afternoon: They would be facing the Redfield Raiders for the first time. I realized that singing was probably just the kids' way of working out some of their heebie-jeebies. (I love that term! It's much more fun than "anxiety," or "apprehension.") But even though I knew it was good for them, I couldn't stand the racket they were making. Suddenly, I had an idea. It was a good one, too, and I acted on it right away. I whistled loudly to get their attention. "Hey, kids," I said. "Let's play chorus. We can take turns being the conductor, okay? I'll go first to show you how."

They looked up at me expectantly. I raised my arms. "First of all, we're going to sing the same song," I said. "And *not* 'Jingle Bells.' It's too hot and muggy to sing Christmas carols. All right, let's try something simple, like — "

Bart raised his hand. "How about 'We're Off To See the Wizard'?" he asked.

"Perfect," I said. "Ready, everyone?" I got them started, and then after two verses I tapped my little brother David Michael on the shoulder. "You conduct now," I whispered to him. He took over, and I leaned back in my seat and sighed. Listening to nine voices singing the *same* song was about a hundred times better than listening to nine different songs.

"Nice going, Kristy," said Bart.

"Yeah," said Charlie from the driver's seat. "Thanks!"

Whew. Once again, I'd had an idea that saved the day. I don't mean to sound conceited, but that happens to me a lot. Getting ideas, I mean. I don't know where they come from; they just pop into my brain all by themselves. My stepfather, Watson Brewer, calls it "the eternal mystery of the creative process." I call it luck.

I guess I should introduce myself. My name's Kristy Thomas (Kristin Amanda Thomas, if you want to be formal), and I'm thirteen and in the eighth grade at Stoneybrook Middle School, which is in the little town of Stoneybrook, Connecticut. I have medium-length brown hair, brown eyes, and I'm short for my age. I'm not one of those girls you sometimes see who look like they stepped out of a fashion magazine. In fact, I'm the opposite of that. I don't care much about how clothes *look*. I just want them to be comfortable. That's why I usually wear jeans and turtlenecks and running shoes.

That Saturday, in the van, it was *way* too hot for jeans and a turtleneck. I was really glad I'd worn shorts and a T-shirt instead. On my T-shirt was written the name of my softball team; it said *Krushers*, in red. Bart was wearing a shirt that looked a lot like it, except his said *Bashers*. That's the name of his team. Some of the kids in the van — Jerry, Joey, Chris, and Patty — are Bashers. The others — David Michael, Buddy, Karen, Jackie, and Nicky — are Krushers. But for that day, all nine kids were Krashers. That's right, Krashers. Bart and I had combined some of the players on each of our teams to make an "all-star" squad that could play teams from other towns. That's why we were traveling the thirty miles to Redfield.

This wasn't the Krashers' first game together. But it was the first one with a new line-up. Bart and I had made some changes and substitutions since the last time the Krashers played. Still, I thought we had a good, strong team. I looked around the crowded van and smiled at the kids as they sang.

Suddenly, I thought of something kind of

funny. Twelve people were in that van, and a *third* of them were in my family! There was Charlie, who's seventeen, and the oldest kid in my family. And there was me. And there was David Michael, my seven-year-old brother. And finally there was Karen Brewer, my stepsister. (She's the one who had been singing "Doe, a deer, a female deer.") She's seven, and a lot of fun. She doesn't live at my house full-time; she and her little brother Andrew live with us only on alternate weekends and for two weeks in the summer. The rest of the time they live with their mother, Watson Brewer's first wife. She's married again, too, to a man named Seth.

I forgot to mention that my family is kind of complicated.

See, my father walked out on my family soon after David Michael was born. He left my mom with four kids to take care of! (I have another brother, named Sam, who's fifteen. He wasn't in the van that day.) My mom's a strong woman, and she hung in there and kept the family going. I really admire her for that. Then, not too long ago, she met Watson Brewer. A nice guy (even though I didn't exactly love him at first sight), with a station wagon and a bald spot on his head. He also happened to be a millionaire! Truth. And so, when they ended up getting married, my family moved into Watson's mansion. It's across town from where I used to live, which is too bad, but it's huge and really comfortable, which is nice.

If the house weren't as big as it is, I don't know what we'd do, because our family just seems to keep growing. First of all, my mom and Watson decided they wanted to bring a baby into our lives, so they adopted a little Vietnamese girl named Emily Michelle. She's two and a half, and incredibly cute. Then, my grandmother Nannie came to live with us, in order to help out with Emily.

We also have a puppy named Shannon, an ancient cat named Boo-Boo, and assorted goldfish. It's a full house, believe me. And you know what? I love it! I like how the house is always full of life, and how we all seem to get along without even trying very hard. It's kind of awesome, really. I also like having lots of little kids around, since taking care of kids is one of my favorite things to do. I love to baby-sit. In fact, I started a club that's all *about* baby-sitting. It's called the Baby-sitters Club (what else could you call it?) and I'm the president. I'll tell you more about the BSC later on.

"Almost there!" sang out Charlie.

"Great," said Bart. "Are you guys ready to play ball?" he asked the kids.

"Yes!" everybody shouted.

"Okay," said Bart. "Kristy and I have worked out the line-up for today. I want you to listen up while she announces it."

I smiled at Bart. It was thoughtful of him to let me read the line-up. And it was nice of him to get the kids' attention for me. Not that I needed his help. I have never had trouble with public speaking. In fact, I'm known for my big mouth and sometimes bossy attitude. I don't love being thought of as bossy, so I try to tone it down, but the good side of it is that I *do* know how to motivate people so that things get done. Luckily, Bart's the kind of guy who isn't intimidated by a person like me. In fact, he thinks I'm special. And I think he's pretty special himself. Uh-oh, am I getting mushy here? I didn't mean to.

As I was saying, I smiled at Bart. Then I picked up my clipboard. "Okay," I said. "Here's the line-up: Buddy at second base, where Matt usually plays." (Buddy Barrett, a Krusher, was substituting for Matt Braddock, who has played second for the Krashers before. Matt's family was away for the weekend.) "David Michael will catch. Jackie, you'll be at shortstop." (Jackie Rodowsky, another Krusher, is known as the Walking Disaster. He's accident-prone, to put it kindly.) "Karen will be in right field, and Nicky will be pitching." (Nicky Pike's a Krusher, and his older sister Mallory is in the BSC.)

I went on to tell the Bashers where they'd be playing. I don't know the kids from Bart's team the way I know the Krushers. I baby-sit all the time for most of the kids on my team, so I know them pretty well. But the Bashers seem like good kids. "Jerry," I said, "you'll be at third. Patty's in center field. Joey's at first, and Chris is in left field." I smiled at everyone. "Got that?" I asked.

They nodded, and just then Charlie called out, "Here we are!" He swung the van into a parking space, and soon we were busy unloading equipment. I led the way to the field, carrying one of our big duffel bags full of bats, balls, and bases.

"Hi, Kristy!" I heard someone calling to me from the sidelines. It was Mary Anne Spier, my best friend and the secretary of the BSC. She was sitting with the other club members, who had come to see the game. I'm lucky to have loyal friends. I waved and smiled, but I was too busy to talk to them just then.

"Kristy, I'm here if you need me!" someone else called. I looked around and saw Jake Kuhn, who had promised to be on hand if we needed a substitute. He was dressed in his Krushers T-shirt, and he looked ready to play.

8

So did Linny and Hannie Papadakis. I also saw a few Bashers in the stands: Dave and Robbie, I think their names were. It was good to know that we'd be covered in case one of our players needed a break.

Our cheerleaders were on hand, too. Or at least two out of three of them were. Vanessa Pike, Nicky and Mallory's sister, was there. So was Charlotte Johanssen, someone we baby-sit for often. But Haley Braddock, Matt's sister, was missing, since she was away with the rest of her family.

I spotted Mr. and Mrs. Pike in the stands, and also Karen and Andrew's mother and stepfather. Andrew was sitting on his mom's lap, and he looked ready to cheer for his big sister.

Soon the game began. I won't bore you with the details, but it turned into a very close and exciting game. The Raiders were a tough team, and they were ahead for the first five innings. I have to say that it didn't look good for the Krashers. I kept glancing at the sky, almost wishing it would rain so that we could avoid losing. A rain-out is better than losing. But even though the skies were as heavy as lead and the humidity level was about 99.9 percent, the rain held off. And it was just as well, since we ended up coming from behind to win the game. (I think it's good to be the underdog sometimes. Winning feels even better when you really have to fight for it.)

After the game, our fans ran onto the field to congratulate us. A few drops of rain had begun to fall, but I didn't mind the sprinkles since I was so hot. "Nice job, Kristy," said Mary Anne, trotting over to me. She was surrounded by the other BSC members: Mallory Pike, Jessi Ramsey, Claudia Kishi, Stacey McGill, and Dawn Schafer.

"Thanks!" I said. "I'm glad you guys were here. Your support really helped." I smiled at my friends. "So, what's everybody doing tonight?"

It turned out that almost everyone had a sitting job. Mary Anne and Mal would be sitting for Mal's sisters and brothers. Claudia was sitting for Jamie and Lucy Newton. And Dawn was sitting for Suzi, Buddy, and Marnie Barrett. Only Stacey and Jessi had the night off. And me? Well, Bart had asked if I'd like to "grab a burger" with him. I don't know if you could call that a date, exactly, but I was looking forward to it. Especially now that we could celebrate another Krashers' victory!

CHAPTER 2

Before I go on, maybe I better tell you more about the BSC and its members. First of all, the BSC is more than a club; it's a business, really. A very successful business. The original idea for it was mine, which is why I'm president. I came up with the idea one evening when my mom was trying to find a sitter for David Michael. This was quite awhile ago, before she married Watson. She made, like, a million calls, but nobody was free (including me). Suddenly I thought, why not have *one* number parents could call and get in touch with a whole *group* of sitters?

Simple idea, right? Well, as Watson says, simple ideas are often the best ones. And the club was a big success from the start. At first we advertised with fliers and the occasional ad in the paper, but now we have plenty of clients. We meet in our vice-president Claudia's room three afternoons a week —

11

Mondays, Wednesdays, and Fridays — from five-thirty to six. During those times, parents can call to set up sitting appointments. Our secretary, Mary Anne, keeps a record book so that we know right away which of us is free. The record book was my idea, too.

So was the club notebook, in which each of us writes up every job we go on. Then we read it every week, and that way we keep up with what's going on with our clients. The notebook is not one of my more popular ideas, since hardly anybody likes to spend her time writing up jobs, but everyone admits that it's very helpful. I, personally, think it's one of the things that contributes to the club's success. Parents know we care when we show up on a job already informed about their children.

What else? Well, we have a treasury which we pay dues into. Dues day is Monday, and Stacey, the treasurer, is the one who collects the money. We use the money to pay Charlie to drive me to meetings (now that I live all the way across town), for special projects, and for our Kid-Kits. What are Kid-Kits? Well, they're these boxes we sometimes bring on jobs. We decorated them, and they're full of toys and games that kids love to play with. The things aren't all new, but they're new to the kids we sit for, so Kid-Kits are always a hit. I hate to tell you who had the idea for them, since you might think I'm starting to sound conceited, but I'll admit that her initials are K.T.

Now that you know a little bit about how the club works, let me tell you more about the members.

Mary Anne Spier, who is, as I mentioned, the club's secretary, is also my best friend in the whole world. She and I have been friends as long as I can remember, and somehow I know that we always *will* be friends. I can just picture us at eighty-five, sitting in rockers on a porch somewhere and exchanging memories of the good old days. At eighty-five, I'll still be a loudmouth, and Mary Anne will probably still be her shy, sensitive self. Friendships are funny, aren't they? You'd never guess that Mary Anne and I would be friends, because we're so different on the surface. Mary Anne doesn't offer her opinion until it's asked for; I never wait to be asked. Mary Anne will break into tears if she hears about a lost puppy; I can hardly *remember* the last time I cried. And Mary Anne always knows the right thing to say to someone who's feeling down, while I might not even notice that she's sad in the first place.

However, we are similar in looks. Mary Anne has brown hair and brown eyes, just like me. Plus, she's on the short side. She cares a little more about clothes and stuff, though, so she dresses differently than I do.

Mary Anne is an only child. She was brought up by her father, since her mother died when Mary Anne was just a baby. I guess there weren't as many single parents around back then, and Mr. Spier had to learn for himself how to raise a child on his own. For a long time, I think he tried too hard. He was very strict with Mary Anne. He controlled how she wore her hair (in braids) and how she dressed (in young-looking outfits) and basically, how she lived her life. But finally, just in the last year or so, he's begun to let her take responsibility for herself. Now Mary Anne chooses her own clothes, and fixes her hair the way she likes to. In fact, she recently had it cut short. Plus, she got a kitten named Tigger, and a boyfriend named Logan Bruno.

Mary Anne got something else recently, too. A bigger family! Her father met up with an ex-girlfriend from his high school days, fell in love with her again, and married her. Mary Anne acquired a stepmother, a stepbrother, and a stepsister. And the best thing was this: the new stepsister was Dawn Schafer, another member of the BSC and Mary Anne's other best friend.

Dawn grew up in California, and only

moved to Stoneybrook when her parents got divorced and her mother decided to return to her hometown. The move wasn't easy for Dawn, but I think meeting Mary Anne and becoming a member of the BSC made it nicer for her. Unfortunately, her little brother Jeff never really made the transition. He ended up moving back to California to live with his dad.

Dawn is a pretty cool person, and I really admire her. She's very self-assured. She doesn't hesitate to speak her mind, yet she manages to do so without putting her foot in her mouth the way I so often do. Dawn is pretty, too, with long blonde hair so light it's almost white, and big blue eyes, and a way of dressing that looks comfortable and elegant at the same time. She has a healthy glow about her, which is probably due to the fact that she doesn't eat red meat and she's a health-food nut.

Dawn is also nutty about ghosts. She can talk forever on the subject of ectoplasm and strange footsteps. And she's convinced that the old, old farmhouse where she and her mom live (and where Mary Anne and her dad now live, too) is haunted. She may be right, since there is a secret passage left over from the days of the Underground Railroad. I could easily imagine that ghosts would love that passage.

Dawn's position in the BSC is alternate officer. That means that she can take over the duties of any other officer who can't come to a meeting.

For example, if Stacey McGill couldn't come one day, Dawn could fill in as treasurer. Stacey doesn't miss many meetings, though. She loves her job as treasurer because: a) she's a math whiz, so it's easy and fun for her, and b) she loves to collect, count, and hoard money! Sometimes we practically have to *beg* her to "release the funds" for a pizza bash.

To me, Stacey looks like a model. Honest! She has medium-length blonde hair, which is curly and wild. She gets it permed, I guess, though I never pay too much attention to beauty details like that. Stacey also *dresses* like a model, in outfits I couldn't even begin to imagine wearing. Like lacy purple leggings with big floral tops, or black miniskirts with little cowboy shoes.

Stacey grew up in New York City, which may explain why she is so sophisticated. She moved to Stoneybrook permanently after her parents got divorced. Stacey lives here with her mother, but she visits her father as often as possible. He still lives in New York. Stacey is an only child, and I think because of that the divorce has been especially hard on her. She often feels pulled back and forth between

16

her mother and father. For example, recently her mother was very sick with pneumonia and Stacey felt she needed to be with her, but she had also promised to attend a special event with her father in New York. At times like those, Stacey tries to please everyone and ends up pleasing nobody. That can't be easy.

The other thing that makes Stacey's life hard is that she has diabetes. That's a life-long disease in which the body doesn't process sugars correctly. What it means for Stacey is that she has to be very, very careful about what she eats (no sweets) and that she has to give herself shots of insulin (which her body doesn't produce the way it should) every single day. If *I* had diabetes, I'd probably complain about it to anyone who would listen, but Stacey hardly ever complains. She just deals with it.

Have I made Stacey sound like a hard luck case? She's not. She's full of fun and always ready to jump into whatever's happening. She's a little boy-crazy, wild about shopping, and a great baby-sitter.

Those last three things would also describe Stacey's best friend, Claudia Kishi. Claudia is Japanese-American, and really gorgeous. She has long black hair, almond-shaped brown eyes, and a beautiful complexion. Like Stacey, she's a wild dresser. But while Stacey's outfits tend to be trendy, Claudia's are better described as — well, as creative, I guess. Claudia's a terrific artist, and she applies her artistic ideas to her clothing. She might wear a hand-painted silk scarf to top off a polka-dotted jumpsuit, for example. Or two handmade papier-mâché earrings that look like little donuts, with a third that looks like a cup of coffee. (Claud has two holes pierced in one ear, and one in the other.)

Claudia is vice-president of the BSC, but just like the vice-president of the country, she doesn't have a *lot* of official duties. She's vice-president mainly because we use her room — and her phone — for our meetings. Claud has a private line, and without it we wouldn't have a club. We could never tie up anyone else's line the way we do hers. She does have one official duty: answering the phone when clients call outside of meeting hours. And she has one *un*official duty: supplying the refreshments for our meetings.

Claud's unofficial duty is a labor of love, since she is the Junk Food Queen of Stoneybrook. And although Claud isn't very good at memorizing things or taking tests (which is why she doesn't get such great marks at school, unlike her older sister Janine who is a true genius), she knows her junk food. She can tell you the ingredients and special properties of every candy bar on the market. She can compare and contrast Doritos and Ruffles. And she could pass a cola taste test with flying colors. She just loves junk food, and she always has plenty of it on hand.

You wouldn't see any of the stuff at first if you walked into her room, though. Why? Because she hides it, since her parents don't approve of it. They don't approve of her taste in reading, either; Claud loves Nancy Drew books, and her parents would rather see her read books that are a little more challenging. So the Snickers bars can often be found nestled in a sock drawer, next to a well-thumbed mystery.

The other club members serve as our junior officers. While the rest of us are thirteen and in the eighth grade, Jessi Ramsey and Mallory Pike are eleven and in the sixth grade. They are both great sitters, but neither of them is allowed to sit at night unless she's sitting for her own family. That's why we call them junior officers, and that's why they take a lot of the afternoon jobs.

I can see Jessi and Mallory being friends at eighty-five, just like Mary Anne and me. There they'll be, on the porch. Mal will be sitting in a rocker, writing in her journal. (She wants to be an author-illustrator of children's books, so she's always writing.) And Jessi will be standing near the porch railing with her foot stretched out on top of it, still limber despite her advanced years. (She's a dedicated ballet student, and never seems to stop stretching and practicing.)

Mallory has curly red hair, glasses, and braces. She sometimes refers to her glasses and braces as "the bane of her existence," a phrase she picked up somewhere which means, basically, that she hates them. She'd like to get contacts, but her parents say she's too young. Fortunately, her braces are the clear kind, so they don't even show much — a fact she has a hard time believing. Mal comes from a gigantic family. She has seven younger brothers and sisters! (I've already told you about two of them; Nicky, who's a Krasher, and Vanessa, who's a cheerleader for the team.)

Jessi's family is much smaller. She has a younger sister and a baby brother. Also, her aunt lives with the family, just to help out. Jessi is black, with beautiful cocoa-colored skin and these long, long ballet-dancer legs. I'm really glad that both she and Mallory are in the club.

Finally, the BSC has two associate members. They don't usually come to meetings, but they're ready to help out whenever we're swamped with too much work. One of them is a girl named Shannon Kilbourne, who lives in my new neighborhood, and the other is Logan Bruno, who happens to be Mary Anne's boyfriend!

There. Now you know everything there is to know about the BSC. And now I can finish telling you about what happened after the game that day. That *fateful* day, as Mallory might say, if she were writing one of her stories.

CHAPTER 3

At the ball field, the rain began to fall harder, and the clouds were growing darker by the minute. The air was heavy, and the sky was turning a funny greenish color. My friends ran for their parents' cars, yelling good-bye as they dashed through the rain. Nicky Pike pulled on my arm. "Kristy," he said, "I'm going to ride home with my parents, okay?"

"Sure, Nicky," I replied. "That van was pretty crowded, wasn't it?"

He nodded.

"Got your glove?" I asked.

He held it up. "Okay, then," I said. "See you soon. Congratulations on a great game!" I gave him a high five, and he ran off toward the Pike station wagon.

Soon only Bart and Charlie and I, plus the rest of the Krashers, were left on the field.

"Let's get our stuff together," I said. "Looks like it's going to start *pouring* any minute now." Charlie left to pull the van around so that we could load it up, and Bart and I started to gather the equipment. The kids ran around pretending to help, but I noticed that most of them were playing, instead. Karen was trying to catch raindrops on her tongue. David Michael, Buddy, and Jerry were running and sliding on the wet grass. Jackie was practicing his batting stance, and Chris and Patty and Joey were playing "monkey in the middle" with one of our softballs.

Bart and I looked at each other, shrugged, and started to load up the van. "Okay," I said, when we were finished. "Let's get going!" Nobody paid attention. The rain was falling more heavily. Bart cupped his hands around his mouth. "Last one in the van is a rotten egg!" he yelled. *That* got them going. The kids piled into the van, jostling each other and calling out dibs on the window seats. Bart and I climbed in last, and as soon as we'd taken a quick head count, Charlie started the van and we were on our way.

Just as we reached the main intersection in Redfield, the storm let loose. I heard a tremendous clap of thunder and saw the sky flash with lightning. Rain *poured* down, making it hard to see through the windshield. Charlie peered ahead, then slowed down, watching for road signs.

In the back of the van, Patty burst into tears. "I'm scared of thunder!" she wailed. I reached my hand over the seat to grab hers.

"It's okay," I said. "We're safe in the van. Safe and dry, in our cozy little van." I was trying to sound soothing, but it wasn't easy. I happen to be a little scared of thunder myself. Well, not thunder, but lightning. I'm old enough to know that thunder can't hurt you, but lightning can. This fear of mine is a deep, dark secret. Everybody thinks I'm fearless, but the truth is that I never feel totally at ease during a thunderstorm. I'm always reading these articles about people being struck by lightning and having their zippers welded shut and stuff, and the idea just scares the daylights out of me. But, because I'm scared of lightning, I've also learned a lot about it. I know how to stay safe during a storm (don't go under a tall tree, for example, since lightning is attracted to the tallest point in a landscape), and it just so happens that one of the safest places you can be is in a car. Because of the rubber tires, I think. So anyway, I felt pretty confident in telling Patty that we were safe.

The rain poured down harder, and the thunder boomed even louder. I saw lightning flash to the ground up ahead, and I winced. Some of the other kids were beginning to whimper a little now, and I felt Karen's hand sneak into mine. She was sitting on one side of me, and Bart was on the other. I turned to him. "Some storm, huh?" I said, trying to sound casual.

He nodded, but he seemed distracted. He was looking ahead, through the windshield. "Charlie," he said, suddenly. "Weren't we supposed to turn right at that light?"

"I don't think so," said Charlie. "Our turn is near a big fence with vines climbing over it. Isn't it? I've been watching for it."

"I saw that fence," said Jackie, who was sitting in the front seat next to Charlie. "It was way back that way." He pointed in the opposite direction.

"Are you sure?" asked Charlie.

"Pretty sure," said Jackie.

"Well, I'm just going to keep going for a mile or so," said Charlie. "Maybe there's another turn we can take."

By this time, we'd left the town of Redfield and were driving along a road with fewer houses. Big trees arched over the road, their branches tossing in the wind. We were practically *crawling* along, since Charlie could hardly see to drive. The windshield wipers just could not keep up with the rain that was washing down over the van. Charlie was hunched over the wheel with his face close to the windshield. "I *think* we can turn up here," he said. He sounded kind of tense, the way he does before his team has a big football game.

By this time, there was an odd silence in the van, broken only by Patty's sniffles and the sound of gasps every time a bolt of lightning lit up the world outside the van. The kids needed to be distracted from the storm. "Hey, how about if we all sing?" I suggested, trying to sound enthusiastic. "Let's do 'Take Me Out to the Ballgame,' okay?" I launched right into it. "Take me out to the ballgame." But nobody joined in. I looked around at the scared little faces. "Don't like that song?" I asked. "Okay, how about another? Jackie, you choose."

"I can't think of any songs," said Jackie quietly. He was gazing out the window.

I gave up, and decided just to sit quietly.

"Hey, Charlie," said Bart. "Maybe we should go back to that little general store we passed awhile ago. They might have a phone, or maybe we could ask for directions."

"Good idea," said Charlie. He slowed down and turned the van around. "How far back was it?" he asked.

"Not too far, I think," said Bart. "It was near that big barn."

By this time we were really in the country.

The woods were deep along the sides of the road, and I hadn't seen another car pass us in quite awhile. I hadn't seen many houses, either. At least the rain had let up a little, enough so we could see out the windows.

"Take a right here!" said Bart, when we came to a crossroads. "I'm pretty sure the store was down this road."

"Okay," said Charlie. "But I don't remember — "

The rest of his sentence was drowned out by a loud clap of thunder. Karen put her hands over her ears, and Patty wailed. Charlie just drove on.

We crossed a little bridge that I didn't remember seeing before, and everybody stared out the windows at the swollen stream that ran beneath it. The water ran up over the creek's banks, wild and wavy and full of foam. I saw a couple of good-sized branches being carried along and realized that the water was moving very fast.

"Wow," said Chris. "Look at that!"

"Forget the stream," said Jackie. "Check out that house!"

"Oooh," said three or four of the kids. I peered out the window to see what they were looking at. A huge, imposing brick house stood high on a hillside. A long drive led to it, winding through clumps of tall trees. There were no flowers in the yard, no clothesline, no birdbath. I thought I saw a few lights on in the house, but somehow it still looked empty and abandoned. I felt a chill run down my spine. There was something creepy about the place.

"Whoa!" said Charlie, breaking into my thoughts. The van came to a sudden stop. "Oh, man, *now* what are we going to do?" he asked. I looked through the windshield and saw what he was talking about. Another stream and another bridge were in front of us. But this stream was out of control, and the bridge was almost completely washed away!

"Go back," said Bart. "Quick! Go back to the other bridge."

But guess what happened when we got back to the other bridge? It wasn't there. We looked silently at the few posts that still stood. It didn't take long to figure out that we were stuck. I tried not to panic. "Okay," I said. "There's no way off this road right now, so we're just going to have to knock on somebody's door and ask to use the phone." I thought of the washed-out bridges. "We might even have to ask if we can spend the night," I went on.

"At the haunted house?" yelped Jackie.

"What haunted house?" I asked.

"The creepy brick one," he said. "That's the

only house on this whole road."

"I'm sure it's not haunted," I said, even though I thought it looked creepy, too. "Anyway, it's our only choice." Charlie had already turned the van around, and within minutes we were driving up that long, twisty driveway.

"Weren't the lights on before?" asked Bart, as we approached the house. It was completely dark.

"I think so," I said. "Hey, look," I added. "There's a little cottage. Maybe we can ask there instead of at the big house." I felt relieved at the sight of the cottage, which was hidden in a grove of pines. It looked much homier than the brick house, although no lights were on.

"Must be the caretaker's house," said Charlie, unfastening his seatbelt. "Coming, Kristy?" he said. "Let's go see who's home."

I followed Charlie to the door of the cottage, and stood aside while he knocked. I was getting soaked by the rain, which was still pouring down, but I was beginning to feel hopeful that soon we'd all be warm and dry. Maybe the owner of the cottage would even give us some hot tea.

Then the door opened.

CHAPTER 4

A man stood in the doorway, looking down at us. He was tall and thin and a little stooped, and he had scraggly gray hair. It was still light enough for me to see that his face was gaunt and his gray eyes had no sparkle. The weird thing was that he just stood there looking at us. He didn't say a word.

I didn't say a word, either. I couldn't. I was speechless.

Luckily, Charlie pulled himself together. "Hello, sir," he said. "We were driving on the road down there," he pointed vaguely across the lawn, "and we got stuck when both of the bridges washed out."

Now, if *I* had been the man answering the door, I probably would have said, "Oh, dear, that's terrible. Why don't you come in and dry off?" But the tall man? He didn't say a word. He just kept looking at us. I felt the hairs at the back of my neck begin to prickle.

"I wonder if we could use your phone?" Charlie asked politely.

"No phone here," said the man. "Nor up at the big house. And even if we did have those confounded contraptions, they wouldn't work anyway. Power's out."

Well! He could talk, after all. He wasn't exactly friendly, but at least he had finally spoken. Then his words sunk in. No phone! We were stuck there — probably for the night — and we wouldn't even be able to call our families. My stomach did a flip-flop. This was not a good situation.

"Is there a phone anywhere around?" asked Charlie. "Maybe we could walk to one."

"Impossible, with the bridges out," said the man shortly.

Charlie glanced at me and grimaced. I knew how he felt. We were in big trouble, and we weren't going to get any help out of this strange old man.

Then he surprised both of us.

"You can stay up at the big house," he said. "I'd have you here, but I see you've got a passel of kids with you, and I don't have the space." He nodded toward the van. I looked over at it and saw eight small faces, plus Bart's, peering out at us.

Maybe the old man wasn't so bad after all. "That's very nice of you, sir," I said. "Does that house belong to you?" I didn't mean to be nosy, but I was awfully curious about why he was able to offer it to us.

"I'm the caretaker," he explained. "Nobody's lived there for ages. I've been taking care of it for — for more years than you've been alive, I'd say." He peered at me, and just then I heard a roll of thunder and the sky lit up for a second. I saw the man's hard, gray eyes looking into mine, and I felt a chill. I shook it off.

"I'm Kristy Thomas," I said. "And this is my brother Charlie. We're very grateful to you." I figured the only way to conquer my nervousness was to act self-confident, and it did seem to help.

"I'll get you some supplies," the man said. And just like that, he disappeared into the cottage, leaving Charlie and me standing alone on the front step. We looked at each other. Charlie raised his eyebrows, and I raised mine. Then I turned to the van and gave Bart the thumbs-up sign, to let him know things were okay. I also pointed to the big house and then laid my cheek on my folded hands, to let him know we'd be sleeping up there. He looked confused for a second, but then he nodded, and turned to tell the kids.

"Here you go," said the man, startling me by reappearing suddenly. His arms were full of blankets. "Take these up there. You'll need them if it gets cold tonight. And here are a couple of flashlights and a lantern." He handed an armload to Charlie and disappeared again. Charlie took the stuff to the van, dashing through the rain that still fell heavily, but I stayed by the door. I was ready for the man when he appeared again.

"Don't have much food here," he said, "but I can spare a little." He handed me a large paper bag and I looked inside it. I saw a jug of water, a loaf of bread, and some apples.

"Thank you very much," I said. My stomach rumbled, and I suddenly realized that I was very hungry. I thought about the burger I'd been planning to order at Renwick's with Bart. It would have been hot and juicy and covered with cheese and pickles and ketchup. My mouth watered. I looked at the apples again and swallowed. They'd be better than nothing, at least.

Charlie had come back to the door. He was dripping with rainwater. "I think we're all set," he said. "We certainly appreciate your help," he added.

"One more thing," said the man. He stepped forward and tossed Charlie a set of keys. "You'll need those to get in." Then he ducked back into the cottage doorway and pulled the door shut. Just as the door was closing, I heard him say, "I'll see you in the morning . . . God willing."

"What is *that* supposed to mean?" I whispered to Charlie. We were still standing on the front step, frozen in place.

"Nothing," said Charlie. "I mean, it's just an expression. Something people say." He frowned briefly, and paused. Then he grabbed the food bag out of my hands. "Come on, let's get going," he said, sounding impatient. I followed him back to the van, trying to put the man's words out of my mind.

We climbed into the van, and as Charlie drove to the big house, through the pouring rain, I filled Bart and the kids in on what was happening. I didn't mention how creepy the man seemed, though. No need to scare anyone. Anyway, he had been perfectly nice to us, letting us stay and giving us all those supplies. He just wasn't overly friendly, and there was no reason he should be. Besides, we had other things to worry about.

"My parents are going to be really, really upset when I don't come home," said Jerry. "Can't we call them?"

"I wish we could," I said. "But there's just no way. We'll get out of here as soon as we can tomorrow morning, but for now we're stuck."

I heard some sniffling from the backseat.

The last thing we needed, I thought, was for the kids to get upset and scared. I tried to sound perky. "We'll have fun!" I said. "It'll be like a slumber party."

"But I don't have any pajamas with me!" wailed Karen. "I want my Ariel pajamas!"

"But guess what," said Bart. "We all get to sleep in our clothes tonight. Won't that be cool?"

"Yea!" yelled several of the kids.

I flashed Bart a grateful look.

"Okay, here we are at our mansion," said Charlie, pulling up to a huge, heavy wooden door. "I think it's the butler's night off, so we'll just have to let ourselves in. Shall we, ladies and gentlemen?" Charlie had put on a silly accent. I smiled as the kids jumped out of the van. Maybe this wouldn't be so bad after all.

We hurried through the rain toward Charlie, who was fitting the key in the lock. The big door opened right away, and we saw an immense hallway spreading out before us. Some of the kids dashed inside. "Hold it!" I said. "We have some stuff to unload. And then I want everyone to stick together until we find our way around."

We brought in the things the caretaker had given us and set in the hall. Then Bart and I began to organize them. Food went in one pile, to be taken to the kitchen. Blankets went

35

in another, to be taken to wherever we were going to sleep. Luckily, enough light was coming in through the big windows so that we could see without flashlights, even though it was a little dim inside the house.

We gathered the kids together and walked through the downstairs rooms. "Wow!" said Charlie, when he saw the living room. "Look at those paintings. I'll bet they're worth a lot."

I was too busy checking out the comfy-looking sofas that were grouped around an immense fireplace. I was trying to figure out if we could sleep on them without ruining the expensive-looking fabric they were upholstered in.

The next room was a formal dining room, with a table twice as big as the one in my house. There were twenty — I counted — chairs with beautiful needlepoint seats set around it, and an elegant silver bowl had been placed in the center of its gleaming surface.

"I bet the kitchen's through there," said Joey, pointing. Sure enough, a big, fancy kitchen adjoined the dining room. I ran to the hallway to retrieve our food. When I returned to the kitchen, the kids were exclaiming over the huge cookstove that stood in one corner.

"They used to burn wood in these," Jackie said to me. "Bart told us. And they'd cook on it."

"There's a gas stove, too," said Charlie, "in case we want to boil water or anything."

Suddenly I noticed that there seemed to be too few kids standing around. "Where's David Michael?" I asked. Nobody answered.

Just then, before I had a chance to freak out, I heard David Michael calling. "Come here, you guys! Check it out!"

We followed the sound of his voice and found him standing in an incredible room. I looked around and saw: floor-to-ceiling shelves full of books, plush rugs, rich brown leather chairs, needlepoint pillows, brass lamps, and — a full-sized pool table! "Wow," I breathed, looking at the smooth green surface, which was surrounded by gleaming dark wood. A chandelier hung over the middle of the pool table, with thousands of crystal droplets that seemed to cascade from a central circle. This mansion was even fancier than Watson's.

"Quite a shack we're stuck in," said Bart with a smile.

"You know, though," said Charlie. "There's something odd about all this." He waved his hand as if to indicate the whole house. "I mean, take a sniff. What do you smell?"

I sniffed. "Nothing," I said.

"Leather," said Karen.

"It's not musty, is what I mean," said Charlie. "And there isn't a speck of dust anywhere. This house is kept up pretty well considering no one lives in it."

"I guess that old man's just a really good caretaker," I said, to cover up the fact that Charlie's words had given me another one of those darn chills. "Anyway," I said, trying to change the subject, "maybe we should have something to eat. I know *I'm* hungry."

Karen had wandered over to a window, and was watching the tree branches toss in the wind outside. The storm seemed to be lasting forever. I walked over to her and put my arm around her shoulder. "Coming?" I asked. I could tell she was feeling upset.

"Okay," she said in a small voice. Her lower lip was trembling. "I guess we really are stuck here." I nodded and gave her a comforting hug. It was going to be a long night.

CHAPTER 5

Saturday

You would think that sitting for the Pike kids would keep you busy enough to take your mind off any worries you might have. Well, in my case, you'd be wrong. Sure, they kept Mal and me busy, but they didn't stop me from worrying. And worrying and worrying...

Mary Anne and Dawn returned from Redfield later than they had planned. They had gotten a ride home with the Pikes, and with the rain coming down so hard the drive had been slow. Plus, they'd had to stop at the supermarket, since Mrs. Pike needed to pick up milk. When she dropped them off at their house, Mrs. Pike reminded Mary Anne about the sitting job that evening.

"I'll be over in about a half hour," replied Mary Anne. "I just want to get into some dry clothes."

Mary Anne and Dawn dashed through the rain to their front porch. They stood there for a few minutes, looking out at the storm. "I've never seen anything like this," said Dawn.

Thunder rumbled loudly, and the sky lit up with distant lightning. "I don't know if I've ever seen it rain quite like this either," Mary Anne replied. "It's *pour*ing." Sheets of water ran off the porch roof, and she held out her hand to feel the cascade.

Dawn was wringing out her long hair, which had gotten soaked during the short run from the Pikes' car to the porch. "I'm going to take a shower," she said, "and get ready for my job at the Barretts'."

"I'll be in in a minute," said Mary Anne. She continued to gaze out at the wet world the front yard had become. Huge puddles were forming everywhere, and the trees tossed in the wind. Most of the flowers in the garden were bent over, pounded by the rain. And the rain kept on coming. It seemed, Mary Anne told me later, as if the rain would never stop.

Finally, Mary Anne went inside. The house was quiet, since her dad and Dawn's mother were out running errands. She headed for her room, took off her wet clothes, and dried her hair with a towel. Then she found a clean pair of jeans and her favorite sweat shirt and put them on. Immediately, she felt cozy and warm. She checked her watch. It was almost time to head for the Pikes'.

Downstairs again, Mary Anne rummaged in the hall closet until she found her father's huge umbrella and her hooded slicker. She was looking for her rain boots when the phone rang.

"I'll get it," called Dawn, who had just come downstairs with a towel wrapped around her head. She answered the phone and talked for a few minutes. Then Mary Anne heard her say, "Hold on a second. I'll ask Mary Anne." Dawn dashed into the hall with a strange look on her face.

"What's the matter?" asked Mary Anne.

"It's Watson Brewer," said Dawn. "He says

41

Kristy and Charlie and everyone haven't come back yet. Watson was expecting them an hour ago, and they haven't called or anything."

"That's strange," said Mary Anne.

"I know. Watson seems pretty worried."

"Oh, I'm sure there's nothing to *worry* about," said Mary Anne. "They probably just got slowed down by the storm. Maybe Charlie pulled over for awhile to wait out the rain."

"I bet that's what happened," said Dawn, sounding relieved. "I'll tell Watson." She went back to the phone.

Mary Anne put on her slicker and her boots. Then she looked at herself in the hall mirror and burst out laughing. "Lucky thing Logan can't see me now," she thought. "See you, Dawn," she called. "Have fun at the Barretts'!" She headed out the door and put up the umbrella. The rain was still pounding down, but at least this time Mary Anne was ready for it. The slicker and boots, as funny as they looked, did do the trick. She walked quickly to the Pikes', dodging puddles and jumping over the streams of water that flowed down either side of the street.

Soon Mary Anne stood on the Pike porch, shaking out her umbrella. She took off her slicker and shook it out, too. Then she knocked on the door. She heard pounding feet inside, and then the door was flung open. The triplets (who are ten years old) stood there, grinning at her.

"Ih, mi nadroj," said Jordan.

"Mi mada," said Adam.

"Mi noryb," said Byron.

Mary Anne looked at them, mystified. "What?" she asked.

They repeated what they'd said, only this time they all spoke at the same time. Their words sounded even more like gobbledygook. Mary Anne shook her head and grinned back at them. "I don't know what you're saying, but it's good to see you guys."

"Hi, Mary Anne," said Mallory, coming into the front hall. "Don't mind these guys. They're talking backward. They've been doing it for hours."

"Ohhh," said Mary Anne, finally understanding. "I get it."

The triplets ran off, shouting, "Eybdoog!"

"Makes them kind of hard to understand," Mary Anne said to Mal.

"I know," said Mal. "But it keeps them busy, and I'm happy for that. Come on in. My parents already left. We're just hanging out until suppertime."

The rest of the Pike kids were in the rec room. Vanessa was sitting on the couch with a notebook in her hand. "Hi, Mary Anne," she said. "Guess what I'm doing."

"Writing?" asked Mary Anne. She knows that Vanessa plans to be a poet one day.

"Yup," said Vanessa. "I'm writing some new cheers for the Krashers. It looks like they're going to be playing lots of games this year, so I thought they should have their own cheers. Want to hear one?"

"Sure," replied Mary Anne.

"Krashers, Krashers, you're okay!" yelled Vanessa. "Hit that ball, make that play!" She beamed at Mary Anne.

"Very nice," said Mary Anne.

"Mary Anne! Mary Anne!" yelled Claire, just as Vanessa began another cheer. "Will you spin the dial for us? We want to play Twister."

Claire, who's five, Margo, who's seven, and Nicky were looking up at Mary Anne with expectant faces. (Remember Nicky? He's a Krasher — the one who went home with his parents that day instead of coming with us in the van.) They had already spread the Twister mat on the floor. "Sure, I will," said Mary Anne.

"While you do that, I'll see what we've got for supper," said Mal.

Mary Anne settled in for a game of Twister.

"I'm going first!" said Claire. "Margo got to go first last time."

Mary Anne saw the potential for a squabble, and decided to head it off. "I'm thinking of a

44

number between one and ten," she said. "Whoever guesses the closest gets to go first." Her method worked very well. By chance, Claire picked four, which was the number Mary Anne had been thinking of. Nicky picked five, and Margo picked nine, so Nicky got the second turn.

"Okay, Claire, are you ready?" asked Mary Anne. She spun the dial. "Left foot, red," she said.

Claire put her right foot on a red circle.

"No, no, no, you dumbhead," said Nicky. "Your *left* foot."

"Your sister is not a dumbhead," said Mary Anne. "Here's a new Twister rule: you have to be nice to each other." Mary Anne can't stand it when people tease or insult or call names. "Claire, try the other foot," she said gently.

Soon Claire, Margo, and Nicky were all tangled up on the mat and giggling like crazy. Mary Anne heard the phone ring, but she figured Mallory would answer it, so she kept on spinning. A few minutes later, Mallory joined Mary Anne in the rec room. "That was Dawn. She was calling from home, because the Barretts canceled their plans." She raised her eyebrows at Mary Anne.

Mary Anne looked at her and saw that Mal was trying to tell her something without let-

45

ting the younger kids hear it. "You mean — "
she said, guessing that Buddy Barrett had not
come home yet, which meant that Bart and
Charlie and I and the other kids were still
missing.

"Right," said Mal. "Dawn told me about
that other call from Watson. He's called again,
twice."

"And there's still no word?" Mary Anne
asked.

Mallory shook her head, looking worried.
"None," she replied.

"Wow," said Mary Anne.

"Mary *Anne*!" said Margo. "Spin!"

Mary Anne spun. "Okay, Nicky," she said.
"Right hand, yellow."

"It's *my* turn, not Nicky's," said Claire.

"Oh, right," said Mary Anne. "Okay, then
you do that." She felt completely distracted,
but she was trying not to show it.

Jordan came into the room then. "Mi yrg-
nuh," he said.

"What?" asked Mary Anne.

Adam and Byron were right behind him.
"Emit rof reppus," said Adam.

Mallory translated. "You're hungry, and
you think it's time for supper?" she asked.

"Sey," said Byron. The triplets cracked up.
So did Claire, Nicky, and Margo, who had
just collapsed in a giggling heap. At that mo-

ment the phone rang again. Mallory ran to answer it, and Mary Anne helped the younger kids put away their game. "Go wash up now," she said. "Then we'll have supper."

Mary Anne headed for the kitchen, where she found Mal hanging up the phone. "That was Claudia," she said. "She's about to go over to the Newtons', but she wanted to let us know that Bart's father just called her."

"Did he know anything?" asked Mary Anne.

Mal shook her head. "No," she said. "He was hoping *she* did."

"Oh, no," said Mary Anne. She was beginning to feel seriously worried. And for the rest of the night, that was the state she was in: seriously worried. All through supper there were phone calls, and by the end of the evening it was clear that the Krashers and I had not made it home through the storm. Watson had alerted the police. The parents of the Krashers were all calling each other. Everybody was waiting to hear that the Krashers had been found. But no word came. And the rain just kept on pouring down.

CHAPTER 6

"Kristy?" I turned to see who was tugging on my sleeve. It was Jackie. We were all in the kitchen at the old mansion, and Bart and Charlie and I were dividing up the food the old man had given us. We'd decided that we should try to save half of it for the morning, even though that meant we were going to stay pretty hungry that night.

"What is it, Jackie?" I asked.

"My mom is going to be really worried about me, isn't she?" Jackie looked as if he were about to burst into tears.

I didn't know what to say. It was true. Our parents were going to be worried sick, and there was nothing we could do about it.

Charlie jumped in. "Jackie, listen to me. All of you kids, come here and listen." The kids gathered around Charlie. Most of them looked scared. I heard sniffles, and saw Karen drag her sleeve across her eyes. "It's true that your parents will be worried," Charlie said. "But here's the thing. They'll all call each other, and when they figure out that *none* of us has come home, they'll know that we're still together. That will make them feel better, especially since they know you're with Kristy and Bart."

Bart and I managed to smile at each other.

"And in the morning, we'll figure out a way to get out of here, and you'll all be home before you know it!" finished Charlie.

"Will my mom make me a cake?" asked Jerry.

"I bet she will," said Charlie. "I bet she'll make you anything you want."

Jerry smiled, and so did a lot of the other kids. Charlie had sounded pretty convincing. Then he added something that made *everyone* smile. "How about if we eat?" he asked. "And then, afterward, we can explore the rest of the house. After all, it's not nearly bedtime. We can't watch TV or go for a drive. What else are we going to do tonight?" Charlie glanced at Bart and me as he spoke, checking to make sure his idea was all right with us. I gave him a nod.

Charlie was turning out to be great. He had done an excellent job driving through all that rain, he'd found us a place to stay after we'd gotten stuck, and now he was being terrific with the kids. I felt awfully grateful. As I mentioned, I'm usually a take-charge person, but this was one time when I was happy to have someone help me out. After all, the little kids weren't the only ones who were feeling scared and worried!

We seated the kids around the big kitchen table and passed out a few slices of apple and a big piece of bread to each of them. Bart and Charlie and I each took one slice of apple and a smaller piece of bread. For a few minutes, nobody said anything.

Then Buddy, who had finished his food quickly, spoke up. "Hey, what's that?" He was pointing at a row of bells, mounted on a wooden plank, next to the kitchen door.

I stood up to look at them more closely. Next to each one was a label, with faded, old-fashioned writing on it. "Morning room. Library. Blue room. Parlor," I read out.

"They must be signals," said Charlie. "For the servants. Like, if the morning room bell rang, they'd know they were wanted in there."

"Awesome," said Joey and Jerry, at the same time.

"So, like, if I was in the library playing pool, and I wanted a peanut-butter-and-honey sandwich," said Jackie, "I'd just ring my little bell and somebody would bring me the sandwich?"

"Something like that," said Charlie. He was smiling. "This really is a pretty amazing old house." He popped one last bite of bread into his mouth. "Well, at least there aren't any dishes to wash!" he said. "How about if we start exploring?" He picked up a flashlight and handed it to me, and then took the lantern, too. "It's not dark yet," he said, "but it will be soon. We may need these."

"Everybody ready?" I asked. "Let's go." I led the way, back through the dining room and out into the front hall. There was a beautiful, sweeping staircase leading upstairs. "Let's not go up there yet," I said. "Let's check out the whole downstairs, first."

"We've already seen the living room and the dining room and the library," said Bart. "What else is there?"

"The other rooms listed by those bells. Like the parlor," I said. "Most old houses had a special room where people entertained company. I'll bet it's this way." I went through a door to the right of the staircase. "See?" I said proudly. We had come into a large, very formal room. Straight-backed sofas with shiny green upholstery sat squarely across from each other. Fancy lace doilies covered their backs and arms. At the windows were heavy, rich-looking draperies. A piano stood in a corner, with a gorgeous paisley shawl laid over it. A framed needlepointed picture hung above the piano. Behind one sofa was a large, low table with a beautiful silver tea set on it. And along the wall was a glass-fronted cabinet full of knick-knacks, such as ivory fans and porcelain figures. Karen and Patty were drawn to it, and immediately sat down in front of it to look over its contents.

Meanwhile, Jackie and Buddy had run to the piano. Jackie started to pound out "Chopsticks," and Buddy joined in on the higher keys.

"Hey, hey, you guys," said Bart. "That's no way to treat somebody else's piano."

"But it's the only song I know," said Jackie. "Shea taught it to me. He can play lots of stuff." Shea is Jackie's older brother. He's nine, and he's been taking piano lessons for quite awhile.

"*I* know how to play," said Joey shyly. "Can I try it?"

"As long as you don't bang on it, I guess it's all right," said Bart.

Joey sat down and began to play a lovely, lilting song.

"That's beautiful," I said, when he'd finished. "What's it called?"

" 'Moonlight Sonata,' " Joey said. "I played it for a recital last year."

"How did you learn to do that?" asked

Karen, who was now standing at Joey's elbow. "That was the prettiest music I ever heard."

Joey laughed. "Thanks," he said. "I learned to do it by practicing a lot, every day."

"When we get back, I might ask Daddy if I can take piano lessons," said Karen.

"Great idea," I said, noticing with relief that she'd said "when," not "if." I smiled at her. Then, suddenly I heard a crash. I whirled around.

Chris, David Michael, and Jerry had been playing with the draperies, trying to figure out how they opened and closed. It had seemed like a safe enough game, so I'd let them go ahead. But, when my back was turned, Jackie had joined them. Jackie, the Walking Disaster? Jackie has a knack for breaking things — vases, lamps, his own limbs. This time, he'd managed to pull one of the drapes down so that it now covered him entirely. He was trying desperately to get out from under it, which made a pretty funny sight. The pile of material was bulging in different spots as he moved against it. He looked like a giant amoeba. Soon, we were all laughing. Even Jackie, who was still trying to find his way out from under the heavy cloth.

Finally, Charlie helped him. "I hope this teaches you to be careful in this house," said Charlie. Suddenly he sounded serious. "Some of the things in here must be very valuable. Let's try to leave the house just as we found it, okay?" He looked around at the kids, and then his gaze returned to Jackie.

Jackie nodded. "I'm sorry," he said. "I didn't mean to — "

"I know," said Charlie, patting Jackie on the shoulder. "It's okay. Hey, Bart, can you help me put this back up?"

I decided it was time to leave the parlor. There *were* a lot of nice, expensive-looking things in that room. "We'll go on upstairs while you guys do that," I said to Bart and Charlie. "Come on up when you're done." I herded the kids out of the parlor and back into the main hall. Then we started up the wide staircase.

I was a little nervous about exploring a new part of the house, so I was glad it was still light enough to see without using a flashlight.

When we reached the top of the stairs we saw a long hallway with several closed doors. "Those must be bedrooms," I said. I tried the first door I came to, and it swung open.

"Wow," said Karen, squeezing into the doorway next to me. "Fancy."

It *was* fancy. There was a big bed with a canopy, a huge chest of drawers, and a fireplace. We crowded into the room. The bedspread was blue, and so was the wallpaper.

"Maybe this is the blue room," I said, thinking again of the bells in the kitchen.

"What's that door?" asked Chris. He walked to a door near the chest of drawers and opened it. "Oh, it's the bathroom," he said. "Come and look at this, you guys!"

We saw a huge old bathtub on feet that looked like big claws. The taps were gold and the spout was shaped like a flower. The bathroom also had a double sink with a mirror over it, and an old-fashioned toilet with a pull-chain to flush with. Another door led out of the bathroom. I opened it, and we found ourselves in a feminine-looking bedroom with pink and white wallpaper. A portrait of a young girl hung over the bed. She was pretty, with dark hair and a sad, sweet smile. A brass nameplate below the painting said *Dorothy*.

"I like her," said Karen, gazing at the portrait.

"This room is boring," said Jackie. He led the way back into the hall and then into a third bedroom. This one had probably belonged to a man. The furnishings were dark and heavy, and the bed, covered with a brown spread, stood solidly along one wall. This room also had a fireplace, and over it hung another portrait. This one was of a man, dressed in a tailcoat and looking very stiff. Jackie stepped closer to it and peered at the brass nameplate under the painting.

Just then, Bart and Charlie joined us. "Who's that guy?" Bart asked.

Jackie gulped. "It says his name is Owen Sawyer," he said in a whisper. He sounded frightened for some reason.

"That makes sense," said Charlie. "I think the name of the road we were on is Sawyer Road."

"Really?" asked Jackie. "Then this must be the Sawyer house!"

"So?" asked Buddy. "What does that mean?"

"It means — " said Jackie, "it means that this house is haunted!"

I heard several kids gasp. "What are you talking about, Jackie?" I asked.

"Shea told me all about it," said Jackie. "I thought it was one of his ghost stories, but maybe it's for real! People have seen all kinds of weird stuff happening here. Lights going on and off in the middle of the night, doors that were locked hanging open, smoke coming from the chimney . . ."

Karen leaned forward. She loves ghost stories. "What else?" she asked.

"Sometimes people see a woman walking around, and they say it's the ghost of a woman who died here," Jackie added. His face was white.

My heart was beating fast, and I knew I should jump in before Jackie said anything else. "I'm sure those stories are nothing more than tales people made up for fun," I said firmly. "After all, there are no such things as ghosts." At least, I thought to myself, I sure *hope* there aren't.

CHAPTER 7

"Kristy's right," said Bart. "Ghosts just don't exist, except in stories."

"But — " said Jackie.

"Hey," said Bart, interrupting him. "Let's finish exploring the house, okay?"

"Yeah," said Buddy. "I want to go up those twisty stairs at the end of the hall."

"Me, too," said Joey.

"I want to go back to Dorothy's room," said Karen.

"Dorothy's room?" I asked.

"The one where her picture is hanging," said Karen. "I want to explore it more."

"So do I," said Patty.

"All right." I was happy to notice that the kids didn't seem to have been scared by Jackie's stories. Of course, I knew that the house couldn't be haunted, so I wasn't scared, either. Not *too* scared, anyway. "Bart, why don't you and Charlie take the boys upstairs? Patty and

58

Karen and I will be in Dorothy's room."

The boys took off down the hall, and I led the girls back to the room with pink and white wallpaper. It really was a pretty room. A lacy white canopy was draped over the bed, and a needlepoint rug with roses all over it was on the floor. Karen ran to a bookcase that was built into a comfortable-looking window seat. "I bet Dorothy read these books all the time," she said. "She probably sat right here, looking out the window." She ran her finger down the row of books. "No Beezus and Ramona," she said.

I laughed. "Those books probably weren't even published when Dorothy lived here," I said. "But look." I pulled out a book. "Here's *Little Women*. It looks like this was one of her favorites. See how the pages are all turned down, as if she had marked them?"

"Neat," said Karen.

Patty had been looking around the rest of the room. "Look what I found in the drawer of her nightstand," she said. She held out her hand. In it lay a heart-shaped silver locket and a little golden key.

I felt weird about snooping around this girl's room. Even if she hadn't lived in the house for years and years, she still deserved some privacy. That was what kept me from trying to pry open the locket. "Pretty," I said. "Better put those things back, though." I glanced up at Dorothy's picture. She seemed to be smiling at me.

"Whoa, whoa," said Karen. "Look what I found!" She held up a leather-bound book. "It was behind the rest of the books. I guess that was her hiding place for it."

I took a look at the book Karen held. In gold letters that were stamped into the red cover, it said, *My Diary*. "Karen, put that back!" I said. "You can't read someone else's diary."

"I couldn't even if I wanted to," said Karen. "It's locked." She showed me the tiny padlock that held it shut.

Patty ran to her. "Do you think this key will open it?" she asked, showing Karen the little gold key. Karen took the key and stuck it into the lock, and the book fell open.

Just then, I heard a loud *bang*, as if a door had slammed shut. We jumped, and Karen glanced up at me with a questioning look in her eyes. "Must have been the boys," I said. I didn't mention that the sound seemed to have come from downstairs instead of upstairs, where the boys had gone. I shivered, and rubbed my arms as if to warm myself. Karen had already gone back to the diary.

"She wrote this when she was eighteen," said Karen, peering at the first page. "And the date is January first, nineteen thirty-five."

"Karen, don't — " I began, but it was too late. I was already hooked. I knew it was wrong to read someone's diary, but my curiosity was getting the better of me. It'll be a history lesson, I thought, trying to justify our snooping.

"Can I use that flashlight, Kristy?" asked Karen. "This old-fashioned writing is hard to read. Maybe a little more light would help."

I gave her the flashlight, and Patty and I leaned over Karen's shoulder as she read the first page. " 'New Year's Day, nineteen thirty-five,' " she read. " 'What an exciting time this is! President Roosevelt says the country will be back on its feet soon, and the Depression won't last much longer.' " Karen stumbled over a few words. "You read it, Kristy," she said. "This handwriting is weird and there are a lot of big words."

She handed me the diary. Hesitantly at first, I began to read out loud. " 'Thank goodness Papa managed to avoid losing all his money and we are able to live the way we have always lived. I am grateful for that, but Papa doesn't understand that money isn't everything to me. I would give it all up — and I *shall* give it all up — to marry W. That is, if he ever proposes. I thought he might last night, when we were at the New Year's Ball, but he did not. I know he loves me, I know it!' "

Karen sighed. "This is *so* romantic."

"Keep going," said Patty.

"Wait a second." I held up a finger. I had thought I'd heard a strange sound, like — like someone crying. But when I listened more closely, I didn't hear a thing. I decided it must have been the wind. "Okay, here goes," I said. Suddenly I couldn't wait to find out what would happen next. I was getting used to the handwriting, so I began reading faster.

"The next entry is on February fifteenth," I said. "The day after Valentine's Day. And listen to this: 'Will proposed last night, over dinner at the hotel. He was so sweet and loving, and of course I accepted. I haven't told Papa yet, though. I just know he'll disapprove. He doesn't think Will is good enough for me. For that matter, he doesn't think *anyone* is good enough for me. Papa loves me, I know that, but sometimes his love is just a little stifling. If only Mama were alive, to balance everything out.' "

I thought of Mary Anne. It sounded as if she and Dorothy had a lot in common.

I kept reading. " 'I do love Will, and I plan to marry him with or without Papa's permission. But part of me wonders if it's the right thing to do. If I marry Will — I mean *when* I do — I'll move from my father's house to his.

Shall I ever be able to do all the things I've dreamed of doing, such as touring Europe and visiting exotic lands? Or will I live out my life as first someone's daughter and then as someone's wife?' "

I paused. "She sounds pretty neat," Karen said. "I wonder if she got to do those things."

"Let's keep reading," I said. "Maybe we'll find out."

I found many entries about Will, but a lot about the other things Dorothy wanted to do, too. Still, she and Will continued to plan their marriage.

" 'Friday, June first,' " I read. " 'A week from now, Will and I will be married. Papa, as I guessed he would do, has forbidden me to marry Will, so we have decided to elope. We will do it on June eighth. The plan is for Will to tell Papa that he is taking me out for dinner. But instead of going to the hotel, we will drive to Maryland, where it is easier to get married without a parent's permission. I am excited and anxious and happy and sad — all at the same time.' "

Karen looked up at me and grinned. "They're going to do it!" she said.

"How romantic," added Patty.

"Wow," I said. "I can't wait to hear how it turned out."

I turned the page. " 'Thursday, June seventh,' " I read. " 'Tomorrow is the big day! I've packed a small suitcase and hidden it in the bushes. I've also written a note to Papa, explaining my actions and telling him that I will always love him, even though I have disobeyed him. I only hope he understands. And I hope Will understands that I do not want to live a housewife's life. We have argued about this many times, but I think and hope that he is beginning to see that I'm serious about this. Well, tomorrow night I will be Mrs. William Blackburn. My new life begins in twenty-four hours.' "

"Wow!" Karen said. "I hope she knows what she's doing. Go on, Kristy! What happened next?"

"Nothing," I said. "I mean, I'm sure something happened. But there are no more entries. I guess we'll never know." I shut the little book and tucked it carefully into its original hiding place.

Karen was gazing up at Dorothy's portrait. "Women didn't have it easy back then, did they?" she asked. "I mean, she wanted to get out of her father's house, and the only way was to marry this guy."

"It doesn't seem fair," agreed Patty. "I just hope she got to travel."

I was lost in thought. I was awfully curious

about Dorothy and about what had happened to her. How could we find out more? Then, suddenly, I heard a tapping noise, and I froze. "What's that?" I whispered.

"It's me," said Bart, coming into the room. "Charlie and the boys are downstairs. We explored the upstairs where the servants' quarters were, and the attic, too. It was pretty awesome. We found all kinds of neat stuff. Anyway, we're having a little snack, since we're already starving again. Come on down!"

The girls and I joined the others in the kitchen. Charlie and Bart were talking about going outside and looking for help. "I can't stand just waiting around anymore," said Charlie. "Maybe we can find a phone, at least."

"No way," I said firmly. "First of all, you can't leave me alone with these kids. And anyway, how would you get across that stream, even on foot?" I peered out the window. "And look, the storm hasn't let up at all. In fact, I think it's gotten worse." It was true. The rain was still pouring down, and the wind was blowing harder than ever.

Charlie and Bart looked at each other and shrugged. "I guess you're right," Charlie admitted. "It's going to be dark soon, too. We'll just have to stick it out."

"Right!" I agreed. "We'll be safe here. At least we're out of the rain." I tried to sound convincing, but I was wondering just how safe we were, in that big old mansion on Sawyer Road.

CHAPTER 8

Saterday

    This just wassnt my nigth.
First of all, I was woried sik about
kristy and bart. Then el got caugth
in the rane and turned green.
(And yelow and pruple.) And
then, to top if all off, Jamee
started to ask all thees hard
questoins. It was reely a ~~dis~~
~~desasterus~~ ~~disastres~~ bad night.

By the time Claudia was ready to leave for her job at the Newtons', she had heard that Bart and Charlie and the kids and I were missing. For a few minutes, she considered canceling her job because she wanted to be available to help if she was needed. After all, she thought, the job was a short one. Mr. and Mrs. Newton were only going out for two hours: from seven to nine.

Then Claudia thought again. She told me later that she tried to imagine "what Kristy would say" if she canceled her job, and she realized it was out of the question. "I knew you'd say it was unprofessional," she told me. "I thought you might even yell at me," she added with a grin.

So, Claudia got ready for her job. First, she ate a sandwich since she figured Jamie and Lucy would already have had dinner. Then she checked herself in the mirror and decided she didn't need to change. She was wearing white knee-length jeans shorts, white Keds, and a tie-dyed T-shirt she'd made the weekend before. It was a beautiful one, with spirals of yellow and green and purple, and she was proud of it. She was also wearing a pair of earrings she'd made from green glass she had found on the beach. The glass had been polished by the waves so it had no sharp edges, and Claud had hung two pieces in little silver cages that now dangled from her ears.

Claudia's sister Janine came into her room just as Claud was ready to leave. "Have you heard any news about Kristy yet?" she asked.

"No," replied Claudia. "Nobody's heard anything. I'm really worried."

"I'm sure they'll be fine," said Janine. "Kristy is very intelligent and resourceful."

Claudia rolled her eyes. Janine seems to think that intelligence can solve any problem. Still, Claud knew that Janine was just trying to make her feel better. "I hope you're right," she said to Janine. "And — thanks."

Claudia ran downstairs and looked out the window. The rain, which had been pouring down for hours, finally seemed to have let up. The sky was still dark with clouds, but looked as if it might start to clear up soon. So Claudia decided to forget about a raincoat and umbrella, and just dash to the Newtons'.

" 'Bye!" she called to her parents, who were in the living room. "If anybody calls, I'm at the Newtons'." Claud had talked to Bart's father and Watson, and to Stacey, Mary Anne, and Dawn. Everybody was in a panic, but they could do nothing except wait for good news.

Claudia headed out the door and down the

street. The Newtons live around the block and across the street from the Kishis, so it's only a two-minute walk. But guess what happened during those two minutes? It started to *pour* again. Within seconds, Claudia was soaked. She broke into a run, and arrived, panting, on the Newtons' porch. "Oh, man," she said, wringing out her hair. She did not have time to go home and change, so she just shrugged and rang the bell.

Jamie flung the door open. He's four years old and one of our favorite kids to sit for, since he's very cute and almost always in a good mood. "Hi, Claudia!" he said. "Hey, you look like a rainbow!"

Claudia was confused until she glanced down at herself. Then she cracked up. Her shorts and sneakers were no longer white. Instead, they were streaked with green and purple and yellow. The dye in her beautiful shirt had run! Claud's legs and arms were streaked with color, too. "Oh, no," she said. "I don't believe it."

Mrs. Newton came to the door, carrying Lucy, Jamie's baby sister. "Oh, dear," she said. "You're soaked, aren't you? Do you want to run home and change?"

"No, I don't want to make you late for your dinner," said Claudia. "I'll call my sister and ask her to bring me some dry clothes." Claudia tiptoed into the kitchen, being careful not to drip any color onto the hall carpet, and called Janine.

The next half hour was so busy that Claudia almost forgot to be worried about me. The Newtons left, after Mrs. Newton put Lucy in her baby seat. "I'd give her to you to hold, but I'm afraid I'd come home to a green baby," she joked to Claudia. Lucy cried for a few minutes after her parents left, but stopped when Janine arrived with Claud's dry clothes. Lucy is always very interested in what's going on around her, and she stared wide-eyed at Janine, who smiled back at her. Jamie, meanwhile, was dancing around and singing "Somewhere Over the Rainbow," although he was messing up the words a little.

"Somewhere, over the rainbow," sang Jamie, "there's a pie."

Claudia thanked Janine and asked her to stay for a few minutes while she changed. Then, as soon as she went into the downstairs bathroom to peel off her wet things, she heard Lucy start to cry again.

"What should I do?" called Janine. For all her intelligence, Janine doesn't know nearly as much about little kids as Claudia does.

"There's probably a box of Cheerios in the

cabinet," called Claudia. "Give her a handful."

"But she's going to get milk all over herself!" called Janine.

Claudia giggled. "Don't give her milk," she replied. "Just dry Cheerios. Babies like to eat them."

Claud hurriedly put on the dry clothes and then stood at the sink, trying to scrub the color off her arms and legs. After a few minutes, she gave up. The dye wasn't going to come off that easily. She headed back to the kitchen. Lucy was happily eating Cheerios, Jamie was still singing, and Janine was looking tired.

"I don't know how you do this all the time," she said. "Taking care of kids is hard work."

"But it's fun, too," said Claudia. Then she showed Janine her arms and legs. "How am I going to get this off?" she asked.

Janine frowned. "I'm sure there's a simple solvent," she said. "I'll go home and research it. What are the particular properties of the dye you used?"

"What?" replied Claudia, bewildered.

"Never mind," said Janine. "I'll figure it out."

As soon as Janine walked out the door, Lucy began to cry again. "You just don't like to see *anybody* leave, do you?" said Claudia, picking her up.

"Can we play Wizard of Oz?" asked Jamie. "You can be Dorothy, and Lucy can be Toto, and I'll be the Cowberry Lion."

Claudia laughed, even though Lucy was still crying. "You mean the Cowardly Lion?" she asked Jamie.

"That's what I said," said Jamie. "Or maybe I want to be the Scarecrow."

Just then, the phone rang. Still carrying the crying Lucy, Claud ran to answer it.

"Hi, Claudia, it's me, Mary Anne," said Mary Anne, sniffling.

"You sound terrible," said Claudia. "Did something happen?"

"No, I'm just so worried. Why don't they call us?"

"I don't know. They will as soon as they can, I guess." Claudia noticed that Jamie was watching her closely. "Um, I should go," she said. "Call me if you hear anything."

"Did something bad happen?" asked Jamie, as soon as Claudia hung up. "You look sad."

"I'm fine," answered Claudia, amazed at how sensitive and perceptive kids can be. She didn't want to scare Jamie by telling him that the Krashers and I were missing. "Everything's okay. Should we start our game?" By that time, Lucy had stopped crying and was playing with one of Claudia's earrings.

"Yea!" said Jamie. "You can still carry Lucy, but just pretend you're Dorothy and she's your little dog."

"All right," said Claud. "Come on, Toto, let's follow the yellow brick road." She began to walk through the downstairs, pretending she was following a path. Jamie ran ahead of her and hid behind one of the chairs in the living room.

When Claudia walked by the chair, Jamie jumped out. "Rahhhrrr!" he cried.

Lucy, startled, began to cry. Then the phone rang again. Claudia ran to answer it. This time, Stacey was calling. She had no news, but she was hoping that Claudia did. It was a short call. When Claudia hung up, Jamie looked at her. "What happened?" he asked again.

This time, Claudia told him about the missing Krashers, trying not to make the situation sound too scary. But Jamie was very concerned. "Where do you think they are?" he asked.

"I don't know," said Claudia. "But as soon as it stops raining, they'll probably find their way home."

"What if it doesn't stop raining for a long, long time?" asked Jamie.

"I'm sure it will stop soon," said Claudia, sounding more confident than she really was.

The phone rang again. It was Dawn. She

and Claudia talked for a few minutes. Then, as they were about to hang up, Claudia thought of something. "Do you think anyone has phoned the hospitals around Redfield?" she asked. "I mean, if they were in an — I mean, if something happened, they might be there," she said, catching herself before she said the word "accident" in front of Jamie.

"That's a good idea," said Dawn.

"I'll try calling around," said Claudia. After she hung up, she called information and got the numbers for three hospitals. Then, even though she knew she shouldn't tie up the Newtons' phone, she called each one quickly. None of them had any information about a van accident. Claudia hung up from the last call, not knowing whether to feel relieved or even more worried. Was no news good news?

Jamie tugged on her arm. "Do you think they're dead?" he asked.

Claudia was shocked. Jamie seemed too young to know much about death. "Oh, no, Jamie," she said. "I'm sure they're not dead."

"But kids *can* die, right?" he asked.

"Well," replied Claudia, "they can. That's true. But it doesn't happen very often."

Jamie asked tough questions throughout the evening. It wasn't easy for Claudia to answer some of them, but she did the best she could. When the Newtons came home, she pulled

Mrs. Newton aside and filled her in on what had happened. Then she headed home and called Stacey. "Want to come over and spend the night?" she asked. "I think I need some company."

CHAPTER 9

I sat down at the kitchen table next to Bart. The kids were waiting while Charlie cut up two apples and divided some bread. I knew the kids must be hungry — I certainly was. It was frustrating to know that I couldn't give them as much food as they needed.

"I want my mommy," said Karen, suddenly. "I'm tired of being in this dumb house. Can't we go home now?"

"I want to go home, too," said Chris, sniffling a little. "I miss Molly. She's my dog. She probably wonders where I am. I bet nobody remembered to feed her."

I realized that the younger kids were probably getting tired and therefore cranky. And the older ones were just plain restless. I closed my eyes and crossed my fingers, wishing that the electricity would come back on. Having lights would make everything so much easier. It was almost dark out by then, but it would be awhile before the kids would be ready to go to sleep. Lights would make entertaining the children a lot simpler. But when I opened my eyes, the kitchen was still dim.

I looked around and noticed that the Krushers were sitting on one side of the table, and Bashers were sitting on the other. Even though they'd played a couple of games together as the Krashers, the kids hadn't really gotten to know each other. Since they live in different neighborhoods, they don't spend much time playing together.

Suddenly, I had a good idea. "Hey, listen," I said. "How about if we get to know each other a little better? I mean, all we know about each other is what we've seen on the ballfield. Like, we know Jerry is an awesome third baseman, and we know we can always count on Patty to get a hit and that Joey and Buddy make great double plays. But how about if we find out more?" The kids looked interested, so I went on. "I'll start by saying a few things about myself," I said, "and then we can go around the circle. Okay?"

Everybody nodded. "Well," I said. "My full name is Kristin Amanda Thomas. My best friend's name is Mary Anne Spier. I like sports and animals, and I *don't* like dressing up, eating cabbage, squirrels, loose teeth, and people who chew with their mouths open." I saw a few smiles. I turned to Patty, who sat to my left, and told her to go ahead.

Patty, who's seven years old, and has bright red hair and freckles and a spunky personality, drew in a breath. "I'm Patty," she said. "I have three brothers and we have a horse named Ginger. When I grow up I want to be a carpenter and ride a motorcycle. After that, I want to be the president of the United States."

"Cool," said Joey and Jackie.

Jerry was next. He's a wiry nine-year-old with curly brown hair and a wicked grin. "I have two pesty little brothers and a dog named Winter. I also have a paper route with my best friend Bonzie. His real name is Jimmy, but we call him Bonzie. I like to build forts in the woods."

We went all the way around the circle, while we sat in the ever-darker kitchen and munched on our pieces of apple. I think the kids had fun. I know I did. I learned all about the kids I didn't know, and I even learned new things about the ones I did know. For example, I hadn't known that Buddy Barrett has an aunt who lives in Alaska. Even my own brother had a few surprises for me: Charlie said he remembered holding me when I was a baby! Bart made me blush by telling everyone that one of his favorite things to do was "be with Kristy."

By the time we'd finished, everyone seemed to feel much closer — as if we were a temporary family. Nobody was sniffling anymore or asking for their mommies. Then Bart suggested that we go back to the room with the pool table and "hang out" there until it was time for bed. Charlie lit a lantern and led the kids down the hall. I heard them talking excitedly about some of the things they'd learned they had in common. Bart and I sat alone for a minute at the table.

"That was fun," said Bart. "It was a great idea."

"Thanks," I said. "I was just trying to pass the time and get everyone's minds off our problems."

"I know, but I think it did more than that. I have a feeling the Krashers will be an even better team after this." Bart gave me a gentle smile and touched my hand. "You're a pretty awesome person, Kristin Amanda Thomas," he said.

I blushed, for the second time in a half hour. Luckily, it was too dark for Bart to see my red cheeks. "Come on," I said, jumping up and grabbing a flashlight. "Let's go see what they're doing." Sometimes I still feel shy around Bart.

When we arrived in the library, we found the kids grouped around one of the big leather chairs. The lantern was set up on a nearby table, casting a bright glow over that part of the room. The rest of the room was in shadow. Jackie, who was sitting in the chair, was holding a large book, and the rest of the kids were reading over his shoulder. "Look what we found!" he said, when he saw Bart and me. "It's a scrapbook full of newspaper clippings. It was on that shelf over there." He pointed to a bookshelf near the fireplace.

"What are the clippings about?" asked Bart. He and I joined the group by the chair.

"They're about the family, the Sawyer family," said Buddy, sounding excited.

"Mostly about what happened to Dorothy," said Karen. "On the night she eloped." She sounded sad.

"What happened?" I asked. I looked over Jackie's shoulder and saw the headline on one of the clippings. *Local Girl Still Missing*, it said.

"She disappeared," said Patty. "On the night of June eighth."

"Oh, my lord," I said. "That was the night she was supposed to elope with Will."

Karen nodded solemnly. "Show her the first clipping," she said to Jackie.

Jackie flipped back a page. *Strange Disappearance During Storm*, read the headline. The story went on to tell how Dorothy Sawyer had disappeared during "the worst electrical storm in local memory," while "torrential rains" flooded the area and the bridges on Sawyer road were washed out. I felt a chill run down my spine. The night Dorothy had disappeared had been a night just like this one.

Jackie went on paging through the clippings, and we all read eagerly. We read interviews with Owen Sawyer in which it was clear that Dorothy's disappearance had all but broken his heart. We read interviews with Will Blackburn. He revealed the secret plans that he and Dorothy had made for that night. We read police reports about the search for Dorothy, and a story about how the detective in charge had declared, finally, that Dorothy must be considered dead. *Sawyer Girl Drowned During Storm*, that headline said.

Dorothy's body had never been recovered, according to the articles, but through interviews and investigation, the detective had decided that Dorothy must have drowned as she tried to cross the swollen, raging creek to meet Will.

"This is so sad," said Patty. "Will was waiting for her, and she never came."

"Sad for her father, too," said Bart. "He lost his daughter because he wouldn't let her marry the man she loved. If he'd only let them get married, they wouldn't have had to elope."

"That's true," I replied. "I feel sorry for him. After all, he didn't want her to die."

"He sure didn't," said Bart. "It sounds like he never was the same after she disappeared."

"Look at this," said Jackie. "It's the last clipping in this book." We stared over his shoulder at the clipping. It was an obituary for Owen Sawyer. He had died on December eighth.

"That's six months to the day after Dorothy disappeared," said Charlie softly.

A neighbor was quoted in the article as saying that Owen Sawyer had died "of a broken heart," after his daughter had disappeared.

"Wow," said Karen. "That is just the saddest thing I ever heard about."

We all stood quietly for a moment, thinking about the tragedy that had taken place in that beautiful house. At least, I *thought* we were all standing there. Then I heard David Michael give a squeal. "Look what I found!" he shouted. He was standing by a big rolltop desk, shining a flashlight into an open drawer.

"David Michael, you shouldn't go snooping in people's desks — " I began, but it was too late. He was running over to us with a small, leather-bound album in his hands.

"It's pictures," he said. "Pictures of Dorothy, and Will, and Owen Sawyer — " He showed us the book.

"Why is Will in here?" asked Bart. "I mean, he wasn't part of the family."

"I bet I know," I said. "I bet Owen Sawyer put this book together after Dorothy disappeared. By then he knew that she loved Will, and maybe this was his way of trying to make up for forbidding her to marry him. He made up this album with pictures of all of them, as if they *were* a family."

"Nice theory, Kristy," said Charlie, grinning at me. "Who knows? You may be right." He peered closely at a picture of Will. "Hey, he looks familiar, doesn't he?"

"I think so, too," said Bart. "But how could he? I mean, he would be an old, old man by now."

I looked at the picture and agreed that Will did appear familiar. "He must look like somebody we all see in Stoneybrook," I said. "Like a guy at the gas station, or a checkout clerk at the supermarket."

David Michael closed the book and yawned. I noticed a couple of the other kids yawning, too. "I think it's about time to settle in for the night," I said. "Maybe we can sleep in this room. Where did we leave all those — " I was about to say "blankets," but just then I heard a loud bang.

"It's the ghost!" yelled Jackie.

Several of the kids screamed.

Charlie grabbed a flashlight and ran in the direction of the bang. He came back a few minutes later, grinning. "No ghost," he said. "It was just the caretaker, checking to see how we're doing."

"Why didn't he come in?" I asked.

"I don't know," said Charlie. "He seems shy or something. As soon as I said we were fine, he disappeared without another word."

I looked around at the kids and saw more than one frightened face. Was Charlie right? Were we "fine"?

CHAPTER 10

The kids were scared all right, but they were also tired. Soon, Karen yawned and rubbed her eyes. Then the other kids started to yawn. Have you ever noticed that yawns are catching? They are. They spread really fast. I found myself yawning, even though I didn't feel very sleepy.

I *should* have been tired. It was almost ten o'clock, according to my watch, and I'd had a long, hard day. But I felt keyed up. I was full of questions about the Sawyer family. I was a little nervous — okay, more than a little — about the possibility of ghosts. And, on top of it all, I was trying to figure out where and how all of us were going to sleep.

"I guess we should get out the blankets," I said to Charlie and Bart. "The kids can sleep in here on the couches and chairs."

"Why?" asked Bart.

"Why?" I repeated. "What do you mean, why?"

"Why sleep all curled up on a chair when there are plenty of beds upstairs, all made up and ready to be slept in?"

I stared at him. He was right, in a way. The beds upstairs *were* made up; the bedrooms had been taken care of as well as the rest of the house. There wasn't a speck of dust on any of the bedroom furniture, and the sheets and blankets looked fresh and clean. But somehow the idea of sleeping in those rooms gave me the creeps. The rooms looked almost as if they were *waiting* for someone, and I was pretty sure it wasn't me and a gang of three-foot-tall softball players. But how could I explain that feeling to Bart? It would sound silly. Still, there was another, more practical reason why we couldn't sleep up there. "I don't think the kids will want to be separated and put in different rooms," I said. "And anyway, I don't think that old man meant for us to sleep in the beds. Why would he have given us blankets?"

Bart nodded. "I guess you're right," he said. He looked around the library. "But I don't think there's enough room for everyone in here. I think maybe we should go back to the living room and spread out on the floor in there. That carpet was really thick. And if everyone's on the floor, we won't hear any squabbling about who gets what chair or couch."

Bart knows a thing or two about kids. "Good point," I said. "Okay," I called out to the kids. "Time to get ready for bed. Let's head for the living room." I led the way with a flashlight, and Charlie brought up the rear with the lantern.

Bart took another flashlight and looked for the blankets, which we had left in the front hall when we first came in.

Soon we were gathered in the living room. "Okay," I said. "Let's spread out the blankets, and then we'll take turns going to the bathroom." The kids spread the blankets all over the floor, and I noticed that the Krushers and Bashers were mixed together now, instead of forming two different groups. I was glad to see that. Joey and David Michael were near one of the couches. Karen and Patty had decided to sleep near the fireplace, even though there was no fire in it. And Jerry, Chris, Buddy, and Jackie had laid out their blankets in a pinwheel shape, with their heads at the center.

I put down a blanket near Karen and Patty for myself.

"No more blankets left," said Bart. "I guess I'll just sleep on one of these chairs."

"Me, too," said Charlie. "I don't expect to get a lot of sleep tonight anyway."

I don't think *anyone* got a lot of sleep. It was a rough night.

First of all, the trips to the bathroom seemed to last forever. We took each kid in turn, lighting our way with a flashlight.

David Michael was upset because he didn't have a toothbrush with him. "But I'm supposed to brush every single night," he said. "No exceptions. You know what Watson says."

"I do," I said. "But tonight you just can't. Think of it as a vacation from brushing."

"Will Watson be mad?" asked David Michael.

"No, I promise he won't," I said, knowing that if — *when* — we were home again, Watson would be so happy to see us that toothbrushing would be the last thing on his mind.

The next bathroom crisis was Patty's. "I can't wash my face without my Little Mermaid washcloth," she said. "I just *can't.*"

"Well," I said, "then you don't have to wash it tonight."

Once the kids were settled on their blankets and I had turned off the lantern and the flashlights, I thought things would quiet down. But I was wrong. "Bart?" I heard Joey call softly. "I need a drink of water." Bart got up, took the flashlight to the bathroom and returned with a cup of water. About five minutes later, there was another soft whisper from Joey. "Bart? I need to go to the bathroom again."

I heard Bart sigh, but he got up and took Joey to the bathroom. Then there were four *more* trips to the bathroom, as Karen, Jerry, Patty, and Chris decided *they* had to go again, too.

After the second round of bathroom trips, silence fell. I breathed a quiet sigh of relief. Then I heard a rustle near me. "Kristy?" It was Karen. She informed me that she couldn't fall asleep without a pillow.

"Take your sneakers and roll them up in your T-shirt or stuff them under your blanket," called Charlie. "That's what we used to do when we were at camp. It makes a good pillow."

There was a flurry of activity as six out of the eight kids made themselves pillows. I noticed that David Michael and Patty had already fallen asleep. "Two down, six to go," I muttered to myself. And about five minutes later, I heard Karen's breathing become deep and regular, and I knew she was asleep, too. "That makes three," I thought, hoping the other five would soon join them.

Then I heard smothered giggles and gasps coming from behind the couch where the four boys were sleeping in a circle. "Shhh!" I said. "Time to go to sleep now." But the giggling continued.

I stood up, walked over to them, and shone a flashlight down on them. "What's going on?" I asked.

"Jackie's teaching us this funny song," said Jerry. "It's about — "

"I don't even want to hear what it's about," I interrupted. "I want you guys to settle down and get some rest." All four boys immediately put their heads down on their pillows and pretended to snore. They snored loudly, with lots of snorts and whistles. Then they burst into giggles again.

"Okay, that's it," said Bart, getting up from his chair. "The next person who makes any noise is going to have to sleep all by himself in the attic."

Absolute silence. I smiled to myself and headed back to my blanket. The silence continued, and I began to feel my body relax. It was quiet enough to hear the rain falling outside, and I realized that the storm must have moved away from us, since I hadn't heard any thunder or lightning in awhile.

I heard some new sounds, though. As the room grew quieter, I could hear creaks and pops all over the house. I knew it was just the house settling — Watson has told me that old houses do that — but the noises were scary anyway. There were times when they sounded exactly like footsteps on the stairs, or doors swinging shut. I closed my eyes tight and thought to myself, "There are no ghosts, there are no ghosts." But then I thought of the portrait of Dorothy, and of the small, sad smile she wore. I couldn't get her face out of my mind.

Dorothy had been eighteen when she died, only five years older than me. She had left her father's house, knowing that doing so would break his heart, and had gone to meet the man she would marry. And then she had drowned in that cold, rushing stream. It was horrible to picture how she must have tried to swim, and how the water must have carried her away. I shook my head, trying to clear away the awful images.

I tried to think about something nice. I thought about Watson's cabin up at Shadow Lake, where my friends and I had gone for vacation once. I thought about the morning sun shimmering on the water, and about walking around the lake together.

Usually, calling up favorite memories makes me relaxed and puts me right to sleep, but this time it didn't work. I was still seeing Dorothy's face in my mind. I lay awake, listening to the breathing around me, until finally I drifted off into a light sleep.

When I woke up again, it was still dark. I groped for the flashlight and checked my watch. It was after midnight. My back was stiff from sleeping on the floor, and I couldn't find a comfortable position. Charlie, who had fallen asleep soon after the kids quieted down, was snoring loudly, and I heard David Michael muttering in his sleep. He often does that.

I stood up and stretched. Then I picked up the flashlight and started to wander around the room, checking on the kids. They all seemed to be sleeping peacefully.

I decided to go back to the library again, so I picked my way around the kids and headed down the hall. I'd become used to the noises in the house by then, and I felt pretty safe.

I shone the flashlight around the library — on the pool table, the bookshelves, and the rolltop desk. Then I crossed to the desk and started to open drawers. I knew I shouldn't. After all, hadn't I told David Michael not to? But the story of Dorothy Sawyer had begun to fascinate me. I *had* to know more.

In the last drawer I opened, I found another scrapbook full of newspaper clippings. These were more recent ones, from the 1940s. They seemed to be a series of stories, all by the same reporter, about the "ghost" of Sawyer Road. The stories were more funny than scary, as if the writer had a sense of humor, and didn't really believe in ghosts. For example, he told a story about a man who had reported seeing a woman in a long, wet bridal gown, walking along the stream. The reporter suggested that the man had been out too late that Saturday night. Then he told stories about people seeing smoke rise from the chimney, but the reporter wondered whether the smoke was in the *viewer's* eyes. It was all lightly done, and I would have thought it was funny, except that these were the same stories Jackie had told us. If there was really nothing to them, why had they been passed around for fifty years?

I turned the page after reading the last article, and found what appeared to be a legal document of some kind. I was looking at it more closely, trying to figure out what it was, when I felt somebody — or some*thing* — standing next to me. The image of Dorothy came to me again, and I almost screamed.

"What's that?" whispered Bart, leaning over my shoulder to look at the document.

"What — what are you doing here?" I asked, relieved and mad all at the same time.

"I couldn't sleep," he said. He was still looking at the document. "Hey, that's a title to this house, made out to William Blackburn. I guess he bought it after Mr. Sawyer died. That's funny. I wonder if he still owns it."

"I wonder if that's why the house is kept up so perfectly," I said, giving a little shiver. "It's as if he expects her to come back to it."

I showed Bart the articles about the "Sawyer Road Ghost," and we talked for awhile longer. Then I yawned, and he yawned, too. We decided to return to the living room and see if we could sleep a little more. After all, the kids would be waking up in a few hours, and who knew what the next day held in store for us?

CHAPTER 11

Saturday

Well, I _should_ be writing in the notebook about my job sitting for the Barretts. Normally I'd probably be telling about how cute Suzi was, and about the latest thing that Marnie has learned how to do, and about Buddy teaching Pow to shake hands or something. But unfortunately, I can't write anything like that, because my job was canceled! Mrs. Barrett sounded awful when she called to let me know about the Krashers.

Dawn knew, of course, that Buddy was missing — along with me and the other Krashers. But she was planning to go to the Barretts' anyway, just in case Mrs. Barrett still wanted a sitter. Then, about ten minutes before she was going to leave the house, Mrs. Barrett called.

"Oh, Dawn," she said. "I'm so glad I caught you before you left."

"Have you heard from Buddy?" Dawn asked eagerly.

There was a pause. "No," said Mrs. Barrett. "No, I haven't." Her voice was shaky.

Dawn felt terrible. "I'm sorry," she said. "I was hoping you were calling with good news."

"I wish I were. But so far I'm just hoping that no news is good news. I know we'll hear something soon. In the meantime, I'm going to cancel my plans for tonight. I don't want to be away from the phone for a second."

"I can understand that," said Dawn. "Would you like me to come over anyway, to help with Suzi and Marnie?" Dawn had been looking forward to keeping busy with baby-sitting that night, since being stuck at home made her feel helpless and left her with nothing to do but worry.

"Thanks for offering, Dawn," said Mrs. Barrett, "but I think we'll be fine. The girls are pretty subdued, and they'll probably fall asleep early. They've had a busy day."

After Dawn hung up, she wandered into the living room where her mom and Richard were reading the evening paper. "I can't stand this," Dawn said, throwing herself down on the couch. "The waiting is driving me crazy."

"I know," said her mother sympathetically. "Maybe it would help if you were busy with something."

"Like what?" asked Dawn. "My sitting job just got canceled."

"Well, you could always clean your room," said her mom, with a smile.

"I'm not *that* desperate," replied Dawn. She and her mom laughed, and Dawn told me later that she was surprised at how good it felt. Then the phone rang, and Dawn jumped up to answer it.

"Hello?" she said eagerly, again hoping to hear good news. But it was Mary Anne, calling from the Pikes' house. There was no news, she said. She was just checking in. She told Dawn she'd be home soon.

Dawn flopped onto the couch again. "This is so frustrating," she said.

Richard looked up from his newspaper. "I'm sure the police are doing everything they can," he said.

"Oh, I know," said Dawn. "But my friend is out there somewhere, along with a bunch of kids that I happen to care about very much. Why can't I just go out and find them?"

Dawn's mom patted her hand. "Soon the storm will be over, honey, and then the search will be a lot easier. I'm sure the police will have good news for us by tomorrow morning."

"Tomorrow *morning*?" repeated Dawn. She jumped up and began to pace around. "I'll never make it till tomorrow morning."

"Calm down, honey," said Dawn's mom. "Sit down, and let me get you some tea."

Dawn sat down, and she drank the tea her mother made for her, but she didn't calm down much. When Mary Anne returned home, she found one very nervous stepsister waiting for her.

"I can't believe we *still* haven't heard from Kristy," said Dawn, pacing up and down by the living room sofa.

"I know," said Mary Anne, who was lying down with a pillow clutched to her chest. "This just isn't like her. Something is very wrong if she's not calling us." A loud clap of thunder boomed outside, and the girls flinched. "If only the storm would end," said Mary Anne.

"It can't go on forever," said Dawn.

The phone rang, and they both dived for it. Mary Anne grabbed it first. "Hello?" she gasped. "Kristy?"

Dawn leaned over and put her ear next to the receiver so she could hear, too.

"No, it's me, Stacey," said the voice on the other end. "I'm just calling to see how you guys are doing. You haven't heard anything, have you?"

"Not a thing," Mary Anne said. "We're going nuts."

"So am I," said Stacey. "And Claud is, too. She's still over at the Newtons', and right now she's doing what she mentioned to Dawn — calling the hospitals to see if — well, just to check."

Mary Anne's eyes grew wide. She knew Stacey had almost said "to see if there's been an accident," and that was something she didn't even want to think about. She was speechless for a second.

Dawn grabbed the phone. "Stace, it's me," she said. "Let us know if Claud finds anything out," she said. "We'll be here, waiting."

"Okay," said Stacey. "I'd better go now. We want to keep the phone lines open, right?"

Dawn hung up and looked at Mary Anne. "Are you okay?" she asked gently. Mary Anne looked as if she were in shock.

100

"Yes," said Mary Anne. "I just hope *they* are."

Dawn didn't have to ask who Mary Anne meant by *they*. "Me, too," she said. She crossed her fingers. Then, just for insurance, she crossed her toes, too. Then she closed her eyes and wished — hard — that the next phone call would be good news.

Now it was Mary Anne's turn to pace. She walked around the sofa and then around the coffee table, making a figure-eight design. Each time she passed the phone, she gave it a Look. Dawn figured that Mary Anne had probably crossed her fingers and toes, too.

"Maybe we should call Watson," said Dawn after awhile. "You know, just to make *sure* he doesn't have any news." She reached for the phone.

Mary Anne stopped her pacing and took the phone from Dawn, gently but firmly. "I'm sure Watson and Kristy's mom are sitting by *their* phone, waiting for it to ring. We don't want to get their hopes up, do we?"

Dawn let go of the phone and Mary Anne hung it up. "I guess you're right," she admitted. Mary Anne began pacing again, and Dawn sat biting her nails.

The phone rang. "That *must* be Kristy!" said Mary Anne. She grabbed the receiver. "Hello?" she said. She listened for a second.

"Oh, hi," she went on, sounding very disappointed. She covered the mouthpiece with her hand. "It's Claudia," she told Dawn.

"Did she find anything out by calling the hospitals?" asked Dawn.

Mary Anne passed the question on. "Nope," she said after she'd listened to Claud for a minute. "Nothing. Anyway, she wants to know if we want to come over and spend the night. Stacey's going, and Claud's also going to call Mallory and Jessi."

"Sure," Dawn said. "We may as well be together, since there's nothing else we can do."

About an hour later, the members of the BSC — with the major exception of yours truly — gathered in Claud's room. Claud had microwaved some popcorn, and she passed it around while everyone talked. They shared stories of where they'd been when they found out that the van was missing. Then they talked about the phone calls that had been made back and forth. They discussed every theory they could think of to explain what had happened to a van full of kids. And they listened to the storm, which was still going on outside.

Nobody got much rest. They spread sleeping bags on Claud's floor and lay down, but they were too tense to sleep. They talked as they waited for the phone to ring. No calls came, though, so they just kept on talking. Finally, though, the room was quiet for awhile. And during that silence, Dawn noticed something. The thunder wasn't booming anymore, and the rain wasn't pounding on the roof. She checked Claud's clock. It was two-thirty A.M. The storm had finally stopped.

When morning came, the sun was shining brightly. "I feel better already," said Dawn, stretching. "I bet we'll hear from Kristy any minute, now that the storm is over."

But the phone didn't ring.

Finally, Mary Anne had had enough waiting. "I'm going to call Kristy's house," she said. And she did, but there was no news. The Krashers and I were still stranded. Mary Anne hung up, looking upset. Then she took a deep breath and tried to smile. "I know," she said. "Let's all write something in the club notebook, so that *when* Kristy comes back she'll know how much we missed her." Mary Anne pulled out the notebook and passed it around. This is what everyone wrote:

Dear Kristy, my best friend forever — I know in my heart that you're okay, but please, please come back soon! I miss you sooooo much.
— Mary Anne

Kristy, I hope you're back soon so I don't have to be president at our next meeting! (Just kidding. Ha, ha.) Seriously, we miss you very much and we're all worried about you and the others.
— Dawn

The BSC isn't the same without you, Kristy. I hope you'll be reading this soon.
— Stacey

I miss you so much that I've even lost my apitite for junk food. There's ~~pryck prakti~~ almost a whole bole of popcorn wateing here for you! — Claudia

All I can say is ditto for what everybody else said. We need our president!   —Mallory

I can't wait to read what you write in the notebook when you get back. Being lost with eight kids has to be the baby-sitting adventure of all time! Hang in there, Kristy.
                                    —Jessi

CHAPTER 12

"Kristy, wake up! Wake up! It's sunny out-side. The storm is over!" Karen was tugging on my right arm, which was hanging off the side of the chair I'd fallen asleep in.

"Okay, okay, I'm awake," I said, yawning and stretching. I opened my eyes and looked out the big window. Karen was right. The sky was bright blue, with puffy white clouds. I rubbed my eyes and looked again. Not a storm cloud in the sky. "All *right*," I said. Not only had we made it through the night, but now it looked as if we might be able to make our way home soon.

"Guess what?" asked Jackie, tugging on my other arm. "The electricity came back on."

"Are you sure?" I asked.

"Yup," he said proudly. "I went around and turned on all the lights, just to see."

"Jackie," I said, "thanks for checking that out. But I think we're wasting power if we leave the lights on, now that it's bright and sunny outside." I smiled at him. "Think you could go back and turn them off?"

"Sure," he replied. "Joey and Chris will help me."

I realized that just about everyone but me had been awake for awhile. I looked around to see if Bart was up, and noticed that the chair he'd been sleeping in was empty. I had been hoping I'd be up before he was, so I could at least scrub my face and try to comb the biggest tangles out of my hair before he laid eyes on me. I don't usually pay lots of attention to my looks, but Charlie and Sam have made sure to let me know that I'm no beauty queen first thing in the morning. I didn't want to scare Bart off.

I stood up and stretched. My body felt stiff and full of kinks, which I decided was normal for someone who has slept in a chair. I tiptoed to the hall, checked one way and then the other, and made a dash for the bathroom, hoping I wouldn't run into Bart on the way. But when I reached the bathroom door, it was closed. Somebody had beat me to it. I waited outside the door, still watching for Bart. Finally, the door swung open, and guess who walked out? Bart himself.

"Morning, Kristy," he said with a smile.

"G' morning," I mumbled. I rushed into the

bathroom and closed the door behind me. Then I checked myself in the mirror. I didn't look bad after all, except for the fact that I was now blushing bright red. I felt silly. I could have been nicer to Bart; at least I could have smiled back at him.

Once I'd scrubbed my face, I headed for the kitchen. I figured everyone would be gathered there, looking for food. We didn't have much left over, but I for one was so hungry that a slice of apple and a piece of stale bread sounded delicious. "Morning, everybody," I said as I entered the room. Just as I'd guessed, all eight kids, plus Bart and Charlie, were seated around the table. Bart was passing out food.

"Hi, Kristy!" said David Michael. "Look what I got!" He held up a crumpled leather object.

"What *is* it?" I asked.

"It's a batting glove," he said. "I traded Joey for it."

"What did *you* get, Joey?" I turned to look at him. Sometimes these "trading sessions" spell disaster. Kids trade away expensive things for junk, and then their parents get mad.

"These cool wristbands!" Joey said, holding up a grubby pair of terry-cloth wristbands decorated with the Mets logo.

"Great trade," I said, relieved. At least David Michael hadn't given away his best pair of sneakers or something. "So," I said, taking a slice of apple and turning to Bart and Charlie. "What's the plan this morning?"

"Well, since the electricity's on, we're hoping we might be able to find a phone that works," said Charlie. "And when I went outside a little while ago, I heard machinery — so I think they've already started to fix the bridges."

I stepped to the window and looked out. There was the van, and there was the caretaker's cottage — and there was the caretaker, himself. He was striding up the driveway toward the big house. "Charlie!" I hissed. "The caretaker's about to knock at the front door!"

Charlie stood up and peered over my shoulder, but the caretaker was already out of sight. Then I heard a knock, just as I'd predicted. Charlie headed for the door, and I was right behind him.

Charlie pulled the big door open. There, on the front step, was the old man. Somehow, in the morning light, he didn't look scary at all. In fact, I had the sudden thought that he looked kind of sad.

"Are the bridges repaired yet?" asked Charlie, without even saying good morning.

"They're working on them," said the caretaker with a smile. "You'll be out of here in no time."

"Good morning," I said, trying to make up for Charlie's lack of manners. But I had an urgent question of my own, so I didn't even wait for the man to respond. Instead, I jumped right in. "Are the phones working?"

"Well, they probably are," said the man. "But it doesn't make much difference. You won't be able to get to a phone until the bridges are fixed."

"Oh, right," I said glumly. "I forgot about that."

"Did you all sleep well?" asked the man, giving Charlie a curious look. I suddenly remembered his strange words as we'd left the cottage the night before. Had they been some kind of warning? Did he know about the Sawyer Road ghost? Had we been in some kind of danger? I looked at the man suspiciously, but Charlie seemed to find nothing out of the ordinary.

"Oh, sure," he said. "We slept fine. We really appreciate your help."

"It was nothing," said the man. "Now, can I help you pack up? You'll probably be able to drive that van out of here fairly soon." Once again, I felt suspicious. Was he trying to get us out of there for some reason?

"Please, come on in," said Charlie. "Kristy,

110

why don't you organize the kids, and I'll round up the blankets and flashlights and things?"

We went into the kitchen. I rounded up the kids and suggested that they gather up their stuff so we could leave as soon as the bridges were fixed. They ran into the living room, and Charlie and I followed them. Bart stayed in the kitchen with the old man.

The living room was full of activity for awhile, as Charlie picked up the blankets and grabbed a team of kids to help him fold them. The other kids were running around scooping up socks and shoes and making sure that they hadn't forgotten anything. Then, I felt someone tugging on my sweat shirt. It was Buddy.

"Kristy?" he said. "You know that man who came in?"

"Uh-huh," I said. "That's the caretaker."

"Well," said Buddy. "I finally figured out who Will Blackburn looks like. You know, Dorothy's fiancé?"

"Hmm?" I said. I was distracted by Karen, who was wailing that she couldn't find her charm bracelet.

"He looks like that man. Like the caretaker," said Buddy.

"*What?*" I asked. "What are you saying?" Suddenly Buddy had my full attention.

"The caretaker. He looks like Will. Or Will

looks like him, I guess," said Buddy.

I pictured Will. Buddy was right! "You know," I said to Buddy. "I think you've got something there." All of a sudden I knew, just *knew* that the caretaker and Will were one and the same person. "Charlie," I said. "Can you help them finish up in here?" I had some detective work to do. I headed back to the kitchen and found Bart and the old man talking about fishing.

"Um, excuse me," I said. "Mr. Blackburn?" I watched the man's face.

"How did you know my name?" he asked.

"Just a hunch," I said. "We found some newspaper articles — "

"Oh, so you think you know the whole story, do you?" Mr. Blackburn said suddenly, sounding fierce. "Well, there's more to it than you can read in the paper."

"There *is*?" I said, leaning toward him. "Can you tell us?"

"It's a sad tale," he said. "About a man who lost the love of his life and never got over it. That man is me. After Dorothy disappeared, I — I — well, I just never really recovered. I bought this house, and I kept it the way it was when Dot — that's what I called her — lived here. I don't know why, except that somehow it's a comfort to me. But I can't bear to live here, amidst all these memories." He gestured, as if to include the whole house. "That's why I live down in the cottage."

Wow. Once he started talking, he had a lot to say! "What about the haunting?" I asked, and held my breath.

"Haunting?" He snorted. "There is no haunting. Those stories are just tales made up by ignorant people looking for amusement."

"But the lights?" I asked. "And the smoke from the chimney?"

"All my doing," he said. "After all, to keep the house this nice, I have to spend some time in here. I don't *mean* to make the place look haunted, but people believe what they want to believe."

By this time, the kids had returned to the kitchen, and they'd caught on immediately. "But what about the ghosts, Mr. Blackburn?" asked Jackie.

"There are no ghosts," said Mr. Blackburn firmly. "Not in this house, not anywhere. Ghosts are merely figments of the imagination."

Jackie looked disappointed.

"Well, I'll be back down at the cottage if you need anything," said Mr. Blackburn, standing up abruptly. Then he smiled at us. "And, by the way, I'd be honored if you'd call me Will." He was out the door before anyone could say anything else.

"Wow!" said Bart. "That's quite a story."

"Sure is," I replied. I turned to Jackie. "Now you can go home and tell Shea that there's no Sawyer Road ghost after all. There *was* a mystery here, but I think we've solved it. It makes a good story, anyway, right?"

Jackie nodded. But he still looked disappointed. I guess he had really been hoping for ghosts.

CHAPTER 13

"There!" said Charlie, dusting off his hands. "I think that's everything." He stood back from the van and nodded. "All packed up and ready to go. Now we just need word that the bridges are fixed."

After Will Blackburn had left, we'd spent about an hour packing up our stuff, tidying the house — in general, making sure we'd be ready to leave the second we heard that we could. I was so eager to get to a phone that I could hardly stand it. I knew that my family and friends — not to mention the families and friends of the Krashers — would be frantic now that morning had come and we were still missing. Missing, without a trace!

If I'd been able to call someone, I might have enjoyed our adventure more. I mean, there we were, spending the night in a supposedly haunted house. We'd uncovered an amazing, tragic story about the people who had lived there. And then we'd actually *met* one of the characters in the story! I knew my friends would be incredibly envious of the experience. Especially Dawn, since there's nothing she loves more than a good ghost story.

But I hadn't enjoyed my adventure, since I was all too aware of the many worried people back in Stoneybrook. And now I had pretty much put the Sawyer mystery behind me. I was just looking forward to being *home*. Anyway, Will had made it clear that the ghost part of the story was nothing *but* a story, so no mystery was left anyway.

Once we'd packed the van, there was nothing else to do. The kids became restless. "When do we get to go home?" whined Karen. Joey and Jerry started to squabble with each other over who should get to play third base in the next Krashers game. David Michael wandered over to the front step, sat down, and put his chin in his hands. He looked bored.

"I think these kids need something to do," Bart whispered to me.

"No joke," I said. "But what can we do around here?"

"See that meadow?" Bart pointed to the left side of the house, where I could see a small meadow filled with wildflowers. "Looks like there's plenty of room there for a ball field. How about it?"

"Great idea!" I said. "We've got all our equipment and everything. But we only have eleven people. How can we play a real game?"

"We can't," said Bart. "But I can hit a lot of balls for fielding practice, and I know a few fun drills we can try, too."

We called the kids over to the van. "How about some softball?" I asked. "Just for fun."

"Yea!" they shouted. We opened the doors of the van, and they jumped in, rummaged around, and came out with mitts, balls, and bats. In five minutes, practice was in full swing.

We had a great time. Bart was in a silly mood, and he hit all kinds of funny balls to the kids: high, high pop-ups, bouncing ground balls, stuff like that. Later, we disguised base-running drills as relay races. The kids loved that. Charlie did, too, and even showed some of the kids how to play "pepper," which is a practice game in which three people alternate batting and catching.

"Whoa!" I heard Charlie call out, as a ball sailed over his head.

"Got it!" I heard someone else say, but I didn't recognize the voice. I turned and saw Will Blackburn dashing across the field. He was pretty quick, for an old guy. He caught the ball bare-handed and held it up, smiling. We gave him a round of applause.

He walked to where Bart and I were standing, and Charlie jogged over, too. Will was panting a little, but he seemed proud of himself for catching the ball. "Guess I still have a little of the center fielder in me," he said. "Used to play for the local team. Forty years ago, that is!"

"Great catch," said Charlie.

"Thanks," said Will. "But I didn't come over here to join your game. I came to let you know that the first bridge is ready for traffic. You can leave any time."

I beamed at Bart, and we gave each other the high five. "Thanks, Mr. Bla — I mean, Will," I said. "Thanks for everything." I turned and cupped my hands around my mouth. "Okay, Krashers!" I yelled. "Let's get going. Next stop, Stoneybrook!" The kids came running.

We said a quick good-bye to Will Blackburn, threw our stuff back into the van, and headed out. Without really meaning to, I held my breath as we passed over the bridge. I guess I didn't trust that it was fixed until we were safely on the other side. The creek was still running fast. The water looked muddy and lots of twigs and small branches were being swept downstream.

"We made it!" cried Karen, as soon as we'd crossed the bridge. "Now we can go home."

"Yea!" yelled the other kids.

Charlie drove on for a few minutes without saying much. I saw his eyes searching the road. Before long, we came to a small general store and Charlie pulled over. "I'll go in and check on directions," he said to me. "Why don't you call home and tell them we're on our way?"

I hadn't noticed the phone booth before he said that, but as soon as I saw it I was out of the car and dialing my home number.

"Watson?" I said, when he answered. "It's me, Kristy. I'm safe and sound — we all are — and we're on our way home. We were stranded in the storm. We should be there within an hour."

"Kristy — " Watson said. His voice sounded strange. Then I heard him gulp, and he spoke again. "We'll be waiting for you," he said, trying to sound calm.

I felt tears come to my eyes. I knew there were tears in Watson's eyes, too. "Will you call the other parents?" I asked.

"You bet I will," said Watson. "It'll be my pleasure."

After we hung up, I ran back to the van. Charlie was already in the driver's seat. "Let's go!" I said. "They're waiting for us!" I was beaming, even though I could still feel a lump in my throat.

"Wait!" said Jerry. "I want to call my mom."

"Me, too," said Joey.

Suddenly a clamor arose from the back seats. Every kid wanted to make a phone call. I understood, but I knew we'd never get going if we had to wait for the kids to tell their parents what was going on. "My stepfather is going to call your parents," I said. "He promised. And the sooner we get going, the sooner we'll be home."

The kids seemed to understand. Charlie started up the van, and we were on our way home. We sang again, just like we had the morning before. (The game against the Raiders seemed like a *week* ago!") We sang the "Tomorrow" song from "Annie." We sang "Happy Days Are Here Again." We sang every happy, upbeat song I could think of. It felt *so* great to know that we'd be home soon.

Less than an hour later, we were back in Stoneybrook. I can't tell you how good it was to drive by the familiar buildings. I was even happy to see my dentist's office. The kids were pointing out landmarks and acting as if they'd been away for months. "There's the library," said Karen, grabbing my hand. "Remember when you took me there and I got out the book about Frog and Toad?"

"Do I remember?" I asked. "I should hope so. It was only two days ago!"

Everybody laughed. Karen pouted for a second, but then she laughed, too. "Hey," she said, in the middle of a giggle. "Look! We're almost at Daddy's house."

Two minutes later, Charlie pulled into our driveway and honked the horn. Watson came striding out of the house to greet us, with my mom and Sam right behind him. And behind *them* was a *huge* crowd of people. I saw Karen's mother, and Buddy's parents, and Mrs. Rodowsky. I saw a whole bunch of Krushers: Margo and Claire Pike, Patsy and Jake Kuhn, and Hannie Papadakis. I saw a lot of adults I didn't know: they must have been Basher parents. Everybody was yelling and grinning and waving their arms around.

Watson and my mom caught me and David Michael and Charlie and Karen in a huge hug. My mom was sniffling, but she was smiling through her tears. "I knew you were all right," she said. "I just had a feeling." She knelt down to hug Karen again. Watson was shaking Charlie's hand, congratulating him on getting us home safely. Sam was pounding Charlie on the back. I looked around at the crowd.

"Kristy!" I heard someone call. "Over here!"

I looked toward the apple tree, and there they were: every other member of the BSC. Mary Anne was waving madly, and Mallory and Jessi were jumping up and down. Claudia, Dawn, and Stacey were holding up a huge banner. *WELLCOME HOME, KRASHERZ!* it said. I knew Claudia must have been responsible for that, since she can't spell to save her life. But, misspelled words and all, the banner was beautiful. I felt tears rolling down my cheeks as I ran to join my friends.

"We didn't want to get in the way of the family reunions," said Mary Anne. "But boy, are we glad to see you." She threw her arms around me. Then everybody else crowded in, and soon we were tangled up in a group hug. That's a BSC tradition, you know.

For the next half hour, everybody wandered around in our yard, hugging and laughing and crying and trading stories. Then, the yard began to clear out as parents took their kids home. I hugged the kids good-bye. I also hugged Bart, and he sneaked in a little kiss. Then I told my friends I'd see them later — we'd decided to have a special meeting of the BSC that afternoon — and went inside to take a shower and have something to eat.

Boy, was I happy to be home. To be in my

own house, with my own stuff. To open the refrigerator and see eight different things that I might want to eat. To lie down on my cozy, comfortable bed, and then to jump up again (I wasn't feeling at all tired, even though I'd barely slept the night before) and take a long, hot shower. Boy.

That afternoon, in Claud's room, I told the other BSC members about our stay in the famous haunted house on Sawyer Road. Just as I'd predicted, Dawn was green with envy. I tried to explain that there was no mystery left, but maybe I wasn't very convincing. That was partly because *I* wasn't totally convinced. Something was nagging at me — something about the story that hadn't been explained. But since I couldn't figure out what it was, I put it out of my head.

The others told me about their night, and about how worried they'd been. Then Claudia proposed that we have a *real* slumber party the following Friday night, to celebrate my return. We thought it was a great idea, and Stacey even agreed to take money out of the treasury for a pizza bash.

That night, as I lay in bed, all I could think of was that line from *The Wizard of Oz*: "There's no place like home. There's no place like home!" For the first time, I really understood what that meant.

CHAPTER 14

"Okay, you guys," I said. "Listen, I think I've got it." Nobody paid any attention. They were all talking at once, and each of them was talking about something different. "Hey, come on!" I said, a little louder. "We have to get this settled." Still no response. The talking and giggling seemed even louder than before.

"Do you guys want pizza or not?" I finally yelled.

That got them. All of a sudden, I had everyone's undivided attention. It was Friday night, and every member of the BSC was at my house for a slumber party. I was about to order pizzas, but I needed to find out what everybody wanted on them. It isn't easy to order pizza for the seven of us; we all have strong feelings about our toppings! I'd spent the last half an hour trying to figure out how to order two large pizzas that would make everyone happy.

"Okay, here goes," I said. "One of the pizzas will have half with sausage — that's for Claudia and me — and half with onions, for Jessi and Dawn. That pizza will also have mushrooms all over it. The other pizza will have half extra cheese and pepperoni, for Mary Anne and Mal, and half plain, for Stacey and anybody else who isn't happy with what they got." I looked around the room. "How does that sound?" I asked. I crossed my fingers, hoping that everyone would agree with what I'd figured out.

"Uh, Kristy?" asked Claudia. "I think you forgot something."

"Oh, no!" I said. "What?"

"The topping we all love the most," said Claud. "Anchovies!" She rolled over on the bed, laughing hysterically. Everybody else cracked up too, including me. Actually I like anchovies, but everybody else hates them.

"Who really eats those things, anyway?" asked Stacey. "I mean, they are totally gross!"

"You know who eats them?" I said. "Sam, that's who!"

Stacey shrieked. She and my brother Sam have had this on-again, off-again romance for awhile. I can't imagine what she sees in him, personally. "Ew, ew, ew!" Stacey was saying. "He really likes them?"

I nodded. I had the feeling that Stacey was re-thinking her relationship with Sam. "He *loves* them," I added, just to rub it in. Then I headed for the kitchen, to phone in our pizza order.

When I returned to my room, I discovered that the others had started to tell ghost stories. The story of my night at the Sawyer house had spread, and ghosts had been a major topic of discussion that week, both in our meetings and at school. The other topic was how brave I, Kristy Thomas, was!

The first I'd heard about it was when Cokie Mason approached me in the hall late Tuesday morning. "Kristy," she said breathlessly, "I hate to admit it, but you are really awesome!"

Now, for Cokie to say something like that — well, it's sort of a miracle. Cokie and I are not friends and we probably never will be. I stared at her. "Well, thanks, Cokie," I said. "That's nice of you to say." Then I started to walk off. I had no idea what she was talking about.

"Kristy, wait," she said, running after me. "I just have to ask you — did you really feel the cold, slimy hand of the ghost just as the clock struck twelve?"

"What?" My first thought was that Cokie had gone crazy. But my second thought was that she had heard about my night at the Sawyer house. Now, I was pretty proud of myself for getting through that night. Not because of ghost stories, but because I'd been responsible

126

for eight kids and they'd all survived. However, I figured that if Cokie wanted to give me credit for being a Ghostbuster, I'd take it. "Uh, yeah, sure I did," I said. "Well, got to run!" I escaped from her as quickly as possible and headed for the cafeteria to meet my friends.

"Dawn," I said, setting my tray down next to her a few minutes later, "I have a feeling you've been telling people about my night in the haunted house." I knew Dawn was responsible, because she's the only one who would make up details like that "cold, slimy hand."

"Um, well — " Dawn began hesitantly. She looked down at her sprout-and-tomato sandwich.

"It's okay," I said. "But you'd better tell me what I supposedly did."

Dawn's eyes lit up. "I guess I might have exaggerated a little," she said. "Or at least, I filled in the details of the story you told us." She grinned at me. "I hope you don't mind," she added.

I didn't mind. It was fun being a hero at school. Anyway, as I walked back into my room after ordering the pizzas that night, I heard Claudia telling a ghost story.

"So then, three days later, the guy goes to the house that the hitchhiking girl had pointed out," she was saying, "and he knocks on the door, and when this woman answers he holds up the sweater." She took a deep breath. "And he tells the woman that her daughter left it in his car."

"Yeah?" asked Dawn eagerly. "And then what?"

Claudia leaned forward. "The woman tells him that her daughter has been dead for fifteen years!"

Everybody gasped.

"She takes him to the cemetery and shows him her daughter's grave," Claudia finished. "Isn't that wild? It's true, too. It happened to my cousin's friend, out on this road near Greenvale." She shuddered.

"Awesome," said Dawn. "I'm going to have to remember that one."

"You should write a book of ghost stories," Mallory said to Dawn. "Claud and I could do the illustrations."

"Great idea," said Mary Anne.

"Maybe I will someday," said Dawn. "For now, it's fun just to tell them — and listen to them — on nights like this."

Half an hour later, we'd finished with ghost stories and had started in on makeovers, when suddenly there was a knock on my bedroom door. "I bet the pizza's here!" I said. I jumped up and opened the door. A delivery boy stood in the hall, holding two boxes of pizza.

"Two large pizzas," he said. "Double anchovies on both!"

My jaw dropped, and I heard my friends squeal. "Anchovies?" I asked.

Sam popped out from behind the delivery boy. "Gotcha!" he cried.

I paid the delivery boy. "How much did he give you to come up here and say that?" I asked. "Just out of curiosity."

"A dollar," the boy said, grinning.

"And there really aren't any anchovies on these pizzas, right?" I asked.

"Nope," he said, still grinning.

I took the pizzas from him and stuck out my tongue at Sam. "Thanks," I said. "See you." I closed my bedroom door behind me and put the pizzas on my desk. We'd already brought paper plates, napkins, and sodas to my room, so we dug right in.

As soon as everybody had grabbed a slice, Claudia held up her hand. "Wait a second," she said. "I think we should have a pizza toast, to Kristy." She held up her slice, point out. "Here's to our president, who survived a night in a haunted house."

"And a night with eight kids," added Mary Anne, holding up *her* slice.

We all held up our slices and bumped the points together. Then we cracked up. It's a silly tradition, but we love it. I took a big bite of my pizza. "Mmm," I said. "This makes up for a night of bread, water, and apples."

"Too bad you didn't have me along on that trip," said Claudia. "I've always got plenty of food with me."

"That is, if you call Doritos 'food,' " said Stacey, smiling.

"Doritos are food!" said Claudia. "They are! I mean, you eat them, right?" She looked as if she was ready to defend Doritos to the death.

Just then, we heard a knock on the door. "Who's there?" I called, hoping it wasn't Sam and the delivery boy again.

"It's me, Karen."

Karen and Andrew were staying at Watson's that weekend. Nannie had promised to keep the little kids out of our hair for the night, and she'd done a great job so far. I glanced at the clock, then opened the door. "Karen, do you know what time it is?" I asked.

She shook her head.

"It's after ten. You should be in bed."

"I know," she said. "Nannie put me to bed, but I couldn't sleep. I keep thinking about Dorothy Sawyer."

"Have you been having bad dreams?" I asked, looking at her closely. Maybe the ghost stories had been too much for her, even though she loves creepy stuff.

130

"No, it's not that," she said. "It's — " She stopped and looked around at my friends, who were listening closely. "It's just that I keep thinking she reminds me of somebody. Don't you think so, too?" Karen held out her hand, palm up. In it was a small picture of Dorothy, one that had been in the album we'd found.

"Karen!" I said. "I can't believe you took that."

"I know I shouldn't have," she said. "I'll send it back."

"And anyway," I said. "Who could she possibly remind you of? Dorothy is dead."

"Not necessarily," said Dawn suddenly. "They never found her body, remember?" Dawn's cheeks were pink, and her eyes sparkled.

I took the picture from Karen and looked at it carefully. My friends crowded around to see it. Then I heard Mary Anne gasp.

"I know her!" she said. I looked at her, and her face was white as a sheet.

"What do you mean?" I asked.

"She's the woman who runs the sewing store downtown. You know, the one where I buy needlepoint patterns sometimes?" Mary Anne took a closer look at the picture. "That's her, I swear!" she said. "Only in this picture she's much, much younger."

"You're right," said Karen. *"That's* who I thought she looked like. I go to that store all the time, with Mommy."

I looked back and forth between Karen and Mary Anne. They seemed so sure about what they were saying. "Well," I said, *"now* what do we do?"

CHAPTER 15

We talked for a long time that night. The possibility that Dorothy Sawyer was actually alive, after all this time, was really awesome.

"You know," I said, at one point, "when I first saw Will Blackburn I thought he looked kind of creepy and mean. But once we got to know him a little bit, I saw that he wasn't so bad. And now that I think about it, he's probably just a really lonely, sad old man."

"So what are you saying?" asked Mary Anne. She could tell I had something on my mind.

"I'm saying that maybe we ought to try to get the two of them together," I said. "Like maybe I should ask Charlie to drive me back to Sawyer Road. I'll tell Will where Dorothy is, and make him happy."

"Whoa," said Stacey. "Not so fast. I mean, what if it isn't really her? He'd be so disappointed."

"It's her," murmured Mary Anne. "I just know it is."

Claudia held out a bag of M&M's, offering them around. "I think it's such a romantic story," she said. "And it *would* be really cool if we could get the two of them together again. But we should be careful, too. For all we know, she could be married to somebody else by now."

We discussed the situation from every angle, and finally decided that we would go to the sewing store to see "Dorothy" the next day. We weren't positive that was what we *should* do, but we were going to do it. Then we went back to doing makeovers, eating tons of junk food, watching a scary old movie on TV, and doing all the other stuff you do at sleepovers. Of course, none of us slept much, but that's typical.

I looked around my room when I woke up the next morning. Mary Anne was still sleeping, in the guest bed next to mine. Mal and Jessi, lying on the floor in sleeping bags, were whispering together as they looked at a book of horse pictures. Claudia and Stacey were sitting at my dressing table, checking out each other's newest lip glosses and trading makeup tips. They were still in pajamas, but their faces were made up as if they were ready for a fancy night out. And Dawn was curled up in my reading chair, dozing, with a half-read magazine in her lap.

"Everybody ready for a trip downtown?" I asked, stretching and yawning. "After we eat breakfast, I mean."

"What's for breakfast?" asked Claudia.

"Watson said he'd make waffles with fruit toppings, and Mom promised to make her special wake-up punch," I said. "It has orange juice and lemonade and all kinds of good stuff mixed together."

"Sounds great," said Mary Anne, rolling over and sitting up. She threw off her blankets. "I'm ready."

"Wait up," said Stacey. "I just want to throw on some real clothes."

"But we're all wearing pajamas," I said. "You don't have to get dressed yet."

"I don't want to take a chance that Sam will see me in these silly things," Stacey said, pulling at her polka-dotted pajamas.

"I guess you decided to forgive him for that anchovy trick," I said, and Stacey blushed.

By the time we had eaten breakfast (Sam didn't show his face at the table — Mom said he'd already left to play basketball with some friends) and gotten dressed, it was almost eleven. Watson had said he would give us a ride downtown whenever we were ready to go. Just before we left, though, I realized that

135

we should call the store first to make sure it was open.

"What's the name of that place, anyway?" I asked Mary Anne. I was flipping through the Yellow Pages.

"Sew Fine," said Mary Anne. "S-E-W, that is. It's near the pet shop."

"Here it is," I said. I grabbed the phone and dialed the number.

"Hello?" A woman answered the phone.

I wondered if it was Dorothy Sawyer. I pictured her holding the phone, looking the way she looked in the big painting in her old room in the house on Sawyer Road.

"Hello?" the woman asked again.

"Oh, uh," I said, "hi. I mean, hello. I mean, I was just calling to see if you're open, but I guess you must be since you picked up the phone, so that's all, I guess, since you do seem to be open." Oh, my lord, how embarrassing. Whoever was on the other end must have thought she was getting a crank call.

The woman laughed. "You're right," she said. "We certainly are open, and we will be until five. Do you need directions?" She sounded nice.

"No, no, that's okay," I said. "Thanks!" I hung up, rolling my eyes. How could I be such a dweeb? I just hoped that by the time we reached the store, the woman would have forgotten all about that phone call. And if she hadn't, I hoped at least that she wouldn't recognize my voice.

We piled into the van. Watson had just started it up when Karen came running out. "Wait for me!" she said. "If you're going to that store, I want to come, too!" She held up the little picture. "I want to find out if that lady really is Dorothy."

"Sure, Karen," I said, feeling bad about not inviting her in the first place. Watson drove downtown and let us off in front of a small store with fabric in the window and a pretty wooden sign with painted letters. "Sew Fine," I read. "It looks like a nice store."

"Oh, it is," said Mary Anne. "They have great stuff here, and they're really friendly and helpful."

"Well?" said Claudia. "What are we waiting for?" She pushed open the door, and we all followed her inside. There was a tinkling of bells as the door closed behind us.

A pleasant-looking elderly woman came out from behind the counter. "Hi there," she said. "Can I help you?" She smiled at us, but she looked a little bewildered at the sight of seven teenagers and one little girl all crowding into that shop at once. Then she spotted Mary Anne. "Why, hello!" she said. "Back for another needlepoint pattern?"

"Uh, no," said Mary Anne. "Actually — "

"We're just here to look," I said, cutting her off. I wasn't quite ready to reveal our reason for coming.

"Oh, you must be the young lady who called earlier," said the woman, turning to smile at me. "I recognize your voice."

I could have died.

She gave me an understanding look. "I hate it when I get flustered on the phone," she said. "Don't you?"

I nodded gratefully. And I decided that, whoever this woman was, she was awfully nice.

"Well, browse as much as you like," she said. "Just let me know if I can help you." She walked back behind the counter and picked up a needlepoint canvas that she was working on.

I walked over to a wall where a million different colors of yarn were displayed on open shelves. Everyone else followed me and clustered around as Karen held out the picture again.

"Do you think it's her?" whispered Jessi. We looked at the picture, then at the woman.

"Definitely," answered Mary Anne, under her breath.

"It sure looks like her," I agreed in a low voice. "So what do we do now?"

138

"You go ask her, Kristy," whispered Stacey.

"Me?" I squeaked.

"Good idea," whispered Claud. "You were the one who was in the house, after all."

"Well, okay," I said. I sneaked another peek at the woman, who seemed to be totally involved in her needlepoint. Karen handed me the picture, and I drew in a big, deep breath. Then I made myself walk over to the counter. The others followed. The woman looked up at me with a questioning smile. I took another breath. "Um," I said, "the real reason we came here today was to ask you something."

She raised her eyebrows.

"I don't know how to put this, so I'll just say it right out. Are you Dorothy Sawyer?"

The woman looked shocked. She didn't speak for a second.

I showed her the picture. "My little sister," I said, pointing at Karen, "found this last weekend. We were out driving and we got stuck between two washed-out bridges, on Sawyer Road. So a man named Will Blackburn let us stay at the big mansion there." I went on and on, telling her our story. She listened without saying a word, although I thought I saw her eyes widen when I mentioned Will's name.

Finally, I finished. She was silent for awhile, and then she started to talk. "You know," she

139

said, "I did love Will, very much."

I gasped. And I heard my friends gasp, too. "So you are — ?" I asked.

"Yes," she said, nodding. "I'm Dorothy Sawyer. At least, I *was*. And, as I said, I did love Will Blackburn. But that night, that stormy, stormy night, when I was swept downstream by the raging creek — " (We were all leaning forward, to catch every word.) " — I realized something. As I was climbing up the muddy bank where I had finally found something to hold onto, I realized that for the first time in my life I was free. Free! I was on my own. I didn't have to answer to any man: not Father, not Will. For, as much as Will loved me, I knew he would have given me the same sort of life that Father had: a life that was overprotected and stifling." Dorothy paused and looked very serious for a moment. "And so I never returned," she went on. "I know it was wrong to let them think I was dead, but it was the only way I could see for me to take control of my life. And take control I did. I made up a new identity for myself. I traveled all over the world. I had a wonderful time. And then, finally, I settled in this little town, near the village of my childhood. Since I've always loved needlework and sewing, I opened this store ten years ago, and I've been here ever since."

I was speechless, and so were my friends. I think we must have stood there staring at her for about five minutes. "Wow," I said finally. "That is an awesome story."

"It's not one I've had the chance to tell too often," she said, smiling.

"But what about Will?" asked Karen all of a sudden. I turned to her, and saw that she looked very sad. "I think he misses you a lot."

Dorothy nodded. "I miss him sometimes, too," she said. "As I said, I've had a good life. But it's been a lonely one, at times."

"Why don't you go see him?" I said, without thinking. "I know he would be happy to know that you're alive. Couldn't you visit him just once?"

Dorothy looked taken aback for a moment. But then she laughed. "Do you know, I think I'll do just that!" she said. "It'll give old Will a turn, but you're right. Now that I know where he is, I think it would be grand to see him."

When my friends and I left the shop that day, we were smiling. Everything had worked out just fine. The Krashers had been marooned, but now we were back. Will Blackburn and Dorothy Sawyer would soon have a happy reunion. And the mystery of the haunted mansion was finally over.

"But I still can't help wondering," said

Dawn, as we walked down the street, "about whether there might be a ghost in that mansion. I mean, what about the things people have seen?"

"Dawn!" I said, "You're really something. You never give up on a ghost story, do you?"

She shook her head happily. "Nope! They're just too much fun."

And in a way, I knew what she meant. I thought of that big old creepy mansion I'd spent the night in, and for a moment I almost wished it *had* been a haunted house. But then I realized that the *real* tale of the Sawyer mansion was better than any ghost story could ever be.

About the Author

ANN M. MARTIN did *a lot* of baby-sitting when she was growing up in Princeton, New Jersey. She is a former editor of books for children, and was graduated from Smith College.

Ms. Martin lives in New York City with her cats, Mouse and Rosie. She likes ice cream and *I Love Lucy*; and she hates to cook.

Ann Martin's Apple Paperbacks include *Yours Turly, Shirley; Ten Kids, No Pets; With You and Without You; Bummer Summer;* and all the other books in the Baby-sitters Club series.

Look for Mystery #10

STACEY AND THE MYSTERY MONEY

I smiled down at Charlotte, and she grinned up at me. "This is Charlotte Johanssen," I said. "I'm baby-sitting her. She's my little sister for the day."

"Maybe she'd like a pair of these stick-on earrings," Betty said, handing them over the counter.

"Oh, they're so cute," said Charlotte, looking at the little pink hearts. "And they match my skirt. But I don't have very much money left."

"Consider them a gift from me," Betty said, smiling. "Here, I'll show you how to put them on." She came out from behind the counter and knelt down in front of Charlotte.

I walked over to the spinner rack to check out the pierced earrings. I had been looking for a pair to go with my purple jumpsuit. Right away, I saw some that looked just right. They were big purple button-shaped earrings with zigzags of pink on them. I held them up to my ears and looked in the mirror. "These are great," I said. I checked the price. Four ninety-five. No problem. I pulled out my wallet and walked back to the counter.

"How do these look?" asked Charlotte, showing me her stick-ons.

"Terrific!" I said. "They look really real. I hope your mother doesn't think I let you get your ears pierced today."

Charlotte giggled. "I feel grown-up in these," she said. "Maybe I'll ask my mom if I can get more, so I can wear them to school."

Betty smiled at me. "Uh-oh," she said. "Looks like I've started something."

I showed her the earrings I wanted and gave her the ten dollar bill I had left to spend.

Betty took it and turned to the register. Then I saw her shoulders stiffen. She turned and gave me a funny look. She looked again at the bill. She rubbed it with her fingers. She held it up to the light. "Stacey," she said in an odd voice. "I think this bill is counterfeit."

#10 *Sea City, Here We Come!*
   The Baby-sitters head back to the Jersey shore for some fun in the sun!

Mysteries:

5 *Mary Anne and the Secret in the Attic*
   Mary Anne discovers a secret about her past and now she's afraid of the future!

6 *The Mystery at Claudia's House*
   Claudia's room has been ransacked! Can the baby-sitters track down whodunnit?

7 *Dawn and the Disappearing Dogs*
   Someone's been stealing dogs all over Stoneybrook!

8 *Jessi and the Jewel Thieves*
   Jessi and her friend Quint are busy tailing two jewel thieves all over the big apple!

9 *Kristy and the Haunted Mansion*
   Kristy and the Krashers are spending the night in a spooky old house!

#10 *Stacey and the Mystery Money*
   Who would give Stacey counterfeit money?

Special Edition (Readers' Request):

Logan's Story
Being a boy baby-sitter isn't easy!